# A. L. TIPPETT

I0593325

# A
# DRAGON'S
# SOUL

## THE MINATH CHRONICLES
### BOOK 3

Copyright © 2022 A. L. Tippett

All rights reserved. This book or parts thereof may not be reproduced in any form, stored in any retrieval system, or transmitted in any form by any means-electronic, mechanical, photocopy, recording, or otherwise-without prior written permission of the publisher.

This is a work of fiction. Names, places, characters and incidents are either the product of the author's imagination or are used fictitiously, and any resemblance to any actual persons, living or dead, organizations, locales or events is entirely coincidental.

Ebook ISBN: 978-0-6488121-3-5
Paperback ISBN: 978-0-6455730-1-5
Cover designed by MiblArt
Published by FireFly Books

FIRE FLY
BOOKS

British spelling and grammar used throughout this book

# CONTENTS

# PROLOGUE

THE SAPPHIRE DRAGON HAD been sleeping for a long time. After the death of her Soulbound all those years ago, she had retreated into a semi-comatose state, only waking once a year to feed. She would have let herself starve to death decades ago, if it weren't for the prophecy. She knew her talent would be needed in the coming battle if her family had any hope of surviving. Blinking her eyes, she sucked in a deep breath and cast her mind out. The tickle of a young woman's magic danced in her mind and a shiver of excitement ran through her body. The woman was a paradox; a stranger and yet, a friend. The smallest spark brightened her gaze, animating her. Licking her lips as she tasted the spice of the woman's magic, she released a small puff of smoke in delight.

The time had finally come. The prophesied one was here.

# CHAPTER ONE

SERA WAS SWIMMING.

No, not swimming. Running. Or rather, trying to. She was wading frantically through thick liquid that had a mind of its own, grabbing at her limbs, trying to drag her into its depths. Darkness pressed in on all sides and drowned her other senses. Faintly, somewhere ahead of her, she could hear an incessant beeping. She frowned and hesitated. Her heart told her that if she continued her struggle towards the high-pitched sound, pain would swiftly follow. Perhaps it would be better to stay here, in this place of darkness. Maybe she should just stop fighting and allow the currents of this strange sea to float her away from the pain and heartache that lay ahead. The tugging around her legs grew more insistent and she automatically dragged her foot forward, fighting the pull. She couldn't give up. Yes, pain waited for her if she followed the sound, but it was better to feel something than to give in to the nothingness that waited for her here. She forged ahead towards the beeping.

Eyelids fluttering, it took a moment for Sera to focus on her surroundings. The constant beeping of a machine monitoring her vitals chimed near her head, exacerbating the headache pounding behind her eyes. Turning her head to locate the medical equipment, she blinked, struggling to read the numbers. Trying to lift her hands to rub the blurriness from her eyes, her heart rate spiked when she realised she was bound to some sort of bed. With a gasp, she pulled feebly at the restraints on her wrists and ankles, whimpering when they remained secure. That slight movement made her hiss at the pain in her ribs. Scanning the room, she took stock of her surroundings. She was laying on a firm mattress with metal bars lining the side — some sort of hospital bed — to which she was shackled. A cannula nestled in the crook of her left arm, hooking her up to a line of fluids. Looking down at herself, she noticed she still wore the guard uniform she'd stolen from the Iniques Rehabilitation Centre. As she moved, her face scratched against her pillow, dried blood crusty on her cheek. She scrunched her brow, trying to remember precisely what had caused it. Running her tongue over her dry lips, she winced at a split on her lower lip. *Well, that answers that question. But how did it happen?* As she continued scanning the room, she realised all her personal belongings had been removed. She could deal without her Personal Security Band and belt pouch but the loss of her blade, Firinne, stung deeply. A small, black security camera was hung conspicuously in the corner of the ceiling, the red light blinking as it watched her. She shifted as the wires from the blood pressure cuff and heart rate monitor on her finger pooled under her left arm uncomfortably. She adjusted the arm's position as best she could, restrained as she was, trying to persuade the wires to move into a straight line from her body to the monitor. The beeping increased in response to her struggles and she grunted at the stabbing pain in her torso. Giving up on her bid to fix them, her eyes traced the wires up to the monitor screen where it sat on a small metal table. The bag of fluids they had hooked her up to was attached to the top of a tall rod connected to the back of the table. Beneath it sat a metal cupboard but Sera had no way of knowing what was hidden inside. The room itself was a stark white box with no decoration or storage. Only one door and a vent in the ceiling for the air conditioning stood out in her assessment.

*Where on Ghaia's good earth am I?*

Shutting her eyes, Sera groaned, frustrated by her lingering grogginess. Struggling to focus, she tried to retrace her steps. Tor, Idris and her, had broken into the Iniques Rehabilitation Centre to save Arius but they'd found her hippogryph Professor, Tormund, instead. They'd wound up battling the IRC guards. She frowned as she wrestled with the hazy details. She'd had to make a kill. But it had all been for nothing. After all that, she'd failed. Arius was still imprisoned and, to add insult to injury, she had been captured too. And she'd lost a friend in the process. Tears fell down her cheeks as she remembered the blood pouring from Tormund's chest.

Her grieving was interrupted by the sound of the solitary door unlocking. Her eyes sprang open and she jerked her head up. The President stepped through the door and locked it behind him with a swipe of his PSB. Turning back to her, he smiled genially and spread his hands wide.

"Sorry about all this, Seraphina. How are you feeling?"

Sera recoiled from the man in front of her. She tried to fling herself from the bed to put as much space as possible between herself and President Kaesus, snarling as she tugged at the shackles around her wrists and ankles. They clanked loudly as she bucked her hips, ignoring the pain in her ribs as she desperately tried to escape the metal bonds. When she finally accepted her efforts were in vain, she slumped back into the mattress in defeat, breathing hard through the pain. Raising her head, she glared at the President, pouring all of her loathing into her gaze. His mouth pulled down. He almost looked sad as he moved closer to her bedside. Sera rejected the thought as soon as it crossed her mind. President Kaesus was self-involved and cruel. He only cared about power and would do anything to keep it all for himself. Her fingers automatically curled into claws and she wished she were free to tear at his face.

"What did you do to my father?" she hissed.

He winced at her words. "Allen is not your biological father," he reminded her gently as he fumbled with something beside her bed. After a moment, the top half of the bed rose to a gentle incline, placing her in an almost seated position.

"He is the man who raised me. He is the man I call Dad. He is my father, no matter what you claim."

President Kaesus slowly reached a hand out, as if he were approaching a wild animal, and began rubbing soothing circles on the back of her hand. She jerked her hand away and tried to tear it out of the cuffs. All she achieved was a raw mark on her skin.

"Don't fucking touch me," she snarled. The hatred threatened to consume her. She'd never felt a rage like this before.

"Allen," the President forced the name through his teeth, "is alive."

Sera's body sagged as relief washed over her. She had hoped he'd only been stunned, but hearing the confirmation lifted a great weight from her heart. "Where is he?" she demanded.

"Allen is here in the high-security block of the IRC as well. Sera, I want you to know that, while I am your true father, I understand he is important to you. I would never hurt someone you cared for." He blinked innocently, but Sera didn't believe him. "You don't seem to realise it yet, but I do care for you, Seraphina. You are my daughter. I didn't even know you existed until recently."

"What about Arius? What did you do to him?"

"Arius? Oh, the dragon." He wrinkled his nose. "If I had raised you, I would have taught you not to place your trust in dragons. Why do you care about him? He was destroying the city. It will take us months to repair the damage he and his companion did."

"He was protecting the city from the black dragon," she ground out. "There may have been some accidental damage along the way, but he saved many lives. Desamor was on a rampage. Who knows what would have happened if Arius and I hadn't fought him."

"Desamor, hey? You seem very familiar with the dragons. What can you tell me about them? Are there others?" He leaned close to her, staring into her eyes. She hadn't realised how lined his face was before now. And that he smelt like pine needles.

Sera snapped her mouth shut and glared at him again, refusing to give away any more information.

He sighed and pulled away from her. After running his fingers through his hair, rumpling the usually carefully arranged style, he began pacing at the foot of her bed. The click of his polished shoes on the tiles echoed through the empty room. Grey strands of hair flecked his temples, shining in the fluorescent light. Sera watched him warily. With another sigh, he stopped and faced her.

"I've always wanted a family." He rubbed his jaw absentmindedly. "I know this is a shock, Seraphina. But I sincerely want us to be... at the very least, friends. I didn't know you were mine until only a few months ago. Do you know what that's like? To go through life, not knowing you have a daughter? And to find out that your ex said the child she bore belonged to another man? And that that daughter is living in the same city as you? I am your father. You are my daughter. I know I have handled things poorly up to this point. In my own way, I was trying to protect you. I don't expect you to understand but I will try—"

"Protect me? Are you fucking serious? Let me tell you right now, building a relationship with your estranged daughter doesn't usually involve imprisoning her!" Sera was shouting now and obstinately ignoring the rapid beeping of the monitor as her heart raced. She struggled against her restraints once again, wincing as her body protested loudly to the ongoing abuse. Stilling her struggles for the sake of her ribs, she settled for baring her teeth in a feral snarl. *How in Ghaia's name did my mother ever wind up with this asshole?*

"If you'd just let me explain—"

"You lost your right to explain anything when you stole my memories of Arius!" Spit flew from her mouth as she raged, but she didn't care.

He spread his hands wide and yelled back at her, "This is why I tied you up! I don't like it any more than you do, but you require medical care!" He paused, pinching the bridge of his nose before taking a few deep breaths to calm down. He pointed at the bag of fluids and his voice softened when he said, "That drip is giving you an intravenous version of Heal. It will help your ribs heal more quickly after the guards cracked two of them. I'm sorry that they hurt you while doing their duty, but I'm trying to fix things now. You would have never allowed me to administer it, if I hadn't restricted your movement." He threw his hands in the air in frustration. "As a bonus, I get to enjoy your undivided attention so I can explain things properly. If I released you, you would instantly leave with your dragon and I would lose my only chance to develop our relationship." He huffed angrily and cracked his neck. "On that note, I can see you're not in the mood to listen and," he glanced at the angry beeping of the monitor and grimaced, "my presence isn't helping you heal. I will leave you alone for now, but I'll have someone drop off some food soon. I imagine you're famished. And I'll send the nurse in now to clean you up and ensure you're comfortable."

Sera stared in bewilderment as the President exited her room. *Why is he pretending to be nice to me now? What purpose does it serve?*

The door opened again almost immediately, and a woman entered. She was pale with plain features and mousy hair that was neither blonde nor brown. Without meeting Sera's gaze, she made a quick note of her vitals on her PSB, replaced the bag of fluids, then checked that there were no bubbles in her drip line. Crouching, she opened the cupboard while Sera tried to peer over her shoulder to identify what was inside. The nurse efficiently located the sterile wipes she was seeking and stood, closing the doors with a bang. Turning back toward the bed, she made an irritated noise in the back of her throat and pulled the wires from where they were still tucked under Sera's arm, straightening them. The nurse clinically wiped Sera's face with a wipe, making Sera wince as she scrubbed the dried blood off. Reaching into a pocket of her gown, she took out a tube of Heal cream and layered it onto the wounds on Sera's face.

Figuring she might be able to convince the nurse to sympathise with her, Sera asked, "Is it true that the drip is giving me another version of Heal to help my ribs? President Kaesus said it was but I don't know whether he's telling me the tru—"

The nurse interrupted brusquely, "The President was correct. You have the latest model of the automatic drip feed to administer the liquid Heal intravenously. No other prisoner receives special treatment in the IRC. But President Kaesus placed specific orders in regards to your care. I will be attending to you three times a day and you will be given meals in the morning and again at night." She sniffed in apparent disgust at Sera being spoiled.

"Oh. That's nice of him, I guess. Do the other prisoners get two meals a day?"

The nurse pursed her lips but didn't answer.

"What's your name, anyway?"

"You can call me, Nurse," she barked. "Prisoners don't get the privilege of knowing the names of the staff. It's protocol."

"Sorry for asking," Sera muttered darkly.

Staring above Sera's head, the nurse asked without inflection, "Do you need to go?"

"I'd love to go. Can you get me out of here? Where are we going?"

The nurse huffed in annoyance and clarified, "No, I meant, do you need to go to the toilet?"

"Oh," Sera said, disappointed. "Erm, yeah, I do actually. Where's the bathroom? Do you have a key for these?" She shook her manacles.

The nurse flashed her a look of derision before masking her emotions once again. "I can't uncuff you. I have a bedpan for you to use. If you can lift your hips, I'll remove your pants and hold it under you."

"I'm not pissing in front of you," Sera said with a grimace.

"You don't have a choice. It's either that or I insert a catheter."

Sera stared at the woman, horrified. Now that her attention had been drawn to it, the pressure in her bladder was hard to ignore. "Fine," she ground out.

The nurse pressed the button to lower her bed into a flat position and pulled a bedpan out from a shelf beneath the bed. A few awkward minutes later, Sera was alone again. She immediately cast her mind out, seeking her Soulbound.

*He has to be here.*

Her mind grazed over the few auras in the cell block. She breathed a sigh of relief when she sensed that of her father.

*Or stepfather, technically. At least, Kaesus was telling the truth about this.* Allen was alive. Locked up like her, but alive. *Thank the Gods.*

He was across the hall from her. She couldn't sense whether he was injured but at least he hadn't been killed when the President shot him. After allowing happiness to fill her heart for a moment she pushed on. As her mind extended outward, she blatantly ignored the President's swirling aura of light and dark and the dim glow of another human. It was probably a guard and she knew she should be paying attention to their patterns in order to plan an escape, but right now she didn't care. She needed to find Arius. Surely, she would have felt it, if something had happened to their connection. She had to keep searching. *Perhaps he was... There.* His aura gave off a dim glow but at least it confirmed he was alive. He was a few doors down to her left and across the hallway. A little whimper escaped Sera's lips as she silently thanked the Four Gods. Brushing her mind against his, she received no response. It felt like he was in his human form but that shouldn't have stopped her from connecting with him. She could only hope he was sleeping to recover his strength. *If the President has drugged him, I'll... I don't know what I'll do.*

As she withdrew, she felt a tug to her right. Another aura pulled at her mind and she followed the feeling. A golden glow, similar to Arius' but softer somehow, enticed her forward. Upon closer inspection, Sera noticed shining blue spots sprinkling the gold. Curious, she inched her consciousness closer.

*Who's there? How did you get into my head?* demanded Elisabeth.

The shock of hearing her mother's voice inside her head sent Sera spinning back into her own mind. The tempo of the monitor's beeping was racing along with her heart. Prickles heated her skin and she panted as if she'd just finished sprinting. The only reason she knew that had been Elisabeth's voice was from hearing her speak in the Seeing Pool. *But how did I manage to connect with her? Since we share the same blood, do we also share the same ability?* Sera shook her head. This was all too weird. *How in the Four Gods' names did I wind up in this situation? Imprisoned by my real father. Hearing the mother I thought was dead for twenty years in my head... Whilst my dragon and my —* she cringed at the word — *stepfather are stuck in this hole with me. I've got to try and save them all but how?*

Despair threatened to overwhelm her. Too much had happened in a too short span of time. She was struggling to save herself, let alone everyone else who needed her. She felt incapable. Useless. Worthless.

*Why me? This isn't fair!*

If she could just punch something, she was sure she'd feel better. She pulled futilely against her restraints once again until giving up and finally allowing the tears to spill from her eyes. Everything ached: her ribs, her face, her heart. She was too tired to fight anymore. Time to sleep. And time to pray that it wouldn't hurt too much when she inevitably died in this prison.

# CHAPTER TWO

THE DOOR SHUT WITH a crisp click, jerking Sera awake. She automatically twisted in her cuffs, anxious to be able to deal with the oncoming threat. Her shoulders relaxed when she recognised the short dark hair and ebony skin of Negotiator Aaron.

"Hi, Tracker Seraphina." He smiled brightly as he tugged a trolley of food to the right side of her bed.

"Aaron!" she exclaimed. "What are you doing here?"

"Bringing you food."

She resisted rolling her eyes but couldn't help muttering, "Obviously." She wriggled on the bed. "What I mean is, why are you here in the IRC bringing me food?"

"When the President asks for your help with a special case, you drop everything and do as he says." He grinned again before concern clouded his expression. "What in Ghaia's name happened? He told me you were aiding the," he glanced around automatically and whispered the word, "dragon that attacked the city. That doesn't seem like something you would do. Talk to me, Sera. I'm here to help."

Sera glared at him suspiciously. It was just like Kaesus to send someone she considered — maybe not a friend, but certainly a close work colleague —to make her spill her secrets.

"I don't talk when I'm bound," she said with a glare and rattled her cuffs, the metal clanking harshly. "Can you release me?" She held up her wrists as best she could, indicating the shackles. "Please," she added as an afterthought.

"I'm sorry, Sera. I'm under strict instructions to keep you here. I wish I could help. But if you cooperate, I'm sure I could speak with the President about removing your bonds."

"Fat chance," she spat. With a groan, she thrashed her head against the pillow in frustration, when a thought suddenly struck her. "If you're visiting me, then you have access to the other prisoners in this building. Do you know how—" her voice caught in her throat as she wondered who to ask about first— "how my father is?" She could still feel Arius' constant presence in the back of her mind so she knew he was at least alive. "Allen Azura. He's in here too and he's hurt. Or at least, he was." She frowned. "How long have I been locked up, anyway?"

"It's been," he checked his PSB and frowned, "two days since the dragon attacked Mandar City. You were captured in the early hours of this morning and have been sleeping for most of the day."

"I wasn't sleeping. I was drugged. Do you know what that feels like, Aaron? To have to fight myself about slipping away into nothingness or forcing myself awake, knowing I'd have to face the pain in both my body and heart when I did so?"

"Sera..." he began awkwardly, "I don't—"

"No," she interrupted. "You don't know. This place is fucked, the system is fucked and the President is the only evil monster in this city. Not the mythics." She turned her head away from him.

There was a pregnant pause when Aaron didn't say anything. Eventually, he pushed the trolley closer. "Here, eat something," he said gently, "and I'll tell you what I can."

Levelling him with a disbelieving stare, she wiggled her shackled wrists again. "I can't," she said drily.

Aaron blushed, "Ah, yes, of course. I forgot, sorry. I have clearance to remove one handcuff so you can eat."

"Is there anything I can say to convince you to take off all my shackles?"

He offered her a sympathetic smile. "I literally only have clearance to remove one." He waved his PSB over her right hand and the shackle sprang open. To prove his point, he waved his PSB over her ankle cuff. Nothing happened.

She sighed and crumpled against her pillow, the brief flash of hope fizzling back into despondency.

The Negotiator pressed a button to lift the head of her bed up so she could sit while she ate. She winced at the ache in her torso as the bed moved. Aaron said, "Sorry, there's no cutlery. They thought you might use them as a weapon. But don't worry, I had them cut it up for you."

She eyed the food tray suspiciously. "I don't want anything," she grumbled.

"Come on, Sera. You must eat something to get your strength up. Are you worried that it's been tampered with?"

She stared at him for a moment, wondering whether to trust him, before nodding mutely.

"Allow me to prove the safety of your dinner." He took the lid off the food with a flourish and the scent of roast pork and vegetables filled her nose. She stifled a moan when she saw there was crackle. Aaron popped a piece of pork into his mouth and closed his eyes. "Scrumptious." He sighed. Until his eyes bugged and he gagged, his hand going for his throat. He began coughing and dragging in laboured breaths. Sera jerked, reaching for him with her free hand but unable to help. She opened her mouth to yell for aid when Aaron's hand covered hers and he grinned mischievously through a mouthful of meat. "Just kidding," he said with a wink. "Your meal is fine. Thanks for sharing."

"Don't do that to me!" she yelled at him.

"Just having some fun. I thought you could do with a laugh."

Sera glared. "I don't want a laugh. I want to know if my family and friends are all safe."

The sparkle in the Negotiator's eyes dwindled and he sobered. "That's fair." He glanced down at his hands awkwardly. "I'm sorry. I was inconsiderate. I was just trying to lighten the mood."

Sera sighed forcefully and lowered her gaze. "It's fine. I understand why you did it. And under other circumstances it would have been funny. But not today." She looked up then, straight into Aaron's eyes, and, in a small voice, said, "You said you wanted me to talk to you? Fine. I'll talk. I'm scared, Aaron. I thought I knew my place in the world. I thought I knew my family. I thought I was working for the good guys. Turns out, I was wrong on all counts. Everything I thought I knew was a lie. My father isn't my father, my dead mother is alive, and dragons aren't extinct." She sat quietly for a moment, pondering how much to tell the Negotiator. He watched her with compassion in his eyes, but it could all be a ploy by Kaesus to gain her trust. She decided on telling him a part of the truth for now. "The only person I can trust right now is Arius. He and I... We're... Suffice to say, I'm not whole without him. Please, tell me he's safe?" She meant to make her question a demand but a sob caught in her throat, ruining the aggressive tone.

"I'm not supposed to talk about the dragon. About Arius," he corrected. He threw a surreptitious glance over his shoulder toward the camera. Picking up the tray with the plate, he balanced it on her lap before pointing at the food. "You eat and I'll talk." Sera complied making Aaron smile before he continued in a whisper. "I haven't seen him myself but I heard the guards talking."

"Squabs," she corrected automatically and smiled at the memory of Wren. *I hope that boy is staying safe.* "A friend of mine called the IRC guards 'squabs,' after squabblers. They're both nasty creatures that nobody likes."

Aaron snorted in amusement. "That's a good name for them." He leant toward her under the guise of adjusting her tray. He murmured, "The squabs are using some experimental drug on Arius to hold him in his human form. Can you believe that? A dragon that can shift into a human!" He shook his head in wonder. "But the side effect is that he's remained unconscious. The President wants to question him but the guards are afraid to wake him in case he burns the place down."

Sera's lips lifted in a half-smile. *Now, there's an idea.*

"I know there are other prisoners in this block, but my brief was only to speak to you. The President thought you'd appreciate a friendly face." He pretended to fluff the pillow behind her head as he whispered in her ear, "But Sera, I want to help you in any way I can, so long as it's within my abilities. Freeing you, I can't do. Even if I wanted to risk it, I don't have the authority to release the rest of your cuffs. But I can keep listening in on the guards and find out what I can about the other prisoners, if you think that will help?"

She nodded and spoke around a mouthful of pork. "Thank you, Aaron." She swallowed and, keeping her eyes on her food, muttered out of the corner of her mouth, "Do you think there's any way you could sneak into Arius' room? If you could unhook him from those drugs..."

He grimaced. "I don't think I can do that. I'm not even sure if I have clearance into his cell." His mouth twisted in response to her disappointed expression. "But I'll keep my eyes and ears open. If there's an opportunity to gently nudge the guards— squabs—" he corrected himself with a shake of his head, "towards unhooking him, I'll do it. Who knows," he grinned, "they might listen to a Negotiator."

# CHAPTER THREE

SHE WAS BORED. SO bored. *Who knew that being a captive to the most powerful man in Mandar would be so dull?*

She'd dozed on and off through the night. And while she lay awake in the darkness with only the faint light of the monitor screen to keep her company, she'd counted the large tiles on the ceiling too many times. There were twenty-four. Her eyes had darted around those same tiles, creating pointless patterns that kept being interrupted by that stupid vent in the middle. Imagining a victorious escape with Arius, her mother and her father helped pass the time, which lead her to mapping out various breakout scenarios in her head, each more unlikely than the last. She'd listened to the constant beeping of the monitor for so long that she thought she could probably mimic that tone and tempo for the rest of her life. *However long that might be.* Since there wasn't a window, she couldn't tell the time, but sometime in the morning, the nurse had come to check her drip again, followed by Aaron, who brought her breakfast. She'd been disappointed when he hadn't been able to offer any further information about the other prisoners. He promised he'd try dig a little deeper before he brought her dinner that night. While she waited impatiently for the time to pass, she cast her mind out once again and sensed her Soulbound, as well as Allen and Elisabeth. She was still blocked from connecting with Arius which frustrated her beyond words. She'd been too afraid to reconnect with her mother's mind.

*It's stupid. I should be ecstatic that I can talk to her.* Sera forced herself to face the fears she'd buried deep inside and analysed why she wasn't trying to connect to her mother. *I'm... afraid. Afraid that she won't be happy to see me. When Kaesus dragged me into her cell, I passed out. Not exactly great daughter material. And I'm so ashamed. She's been rotting in this place nearly my whole life. And I had no idea. I could have saved her. I should have known that my mother was in trouble. I should have found a way to help get her out.*

The door opening disrupted her thoughts. She frowned at the intrusion, wondering who it could be. She flinched when the dark hair and navy suit of the President appeared in the gap. His icy blue eyes fell on her and narrowed at her reaction.

"For fuck's sake," he shouted and slammed the door closed. "I'm not some monster. I'm not one of those rogue mythics you used to track. Why are you still scared of me?"

Sera kept her voice low in contrast to his rage but laced every word with power. "You are so caught up in your plans to dominate the other creatures sharing our world, that you just can't see it. You can't see what you're really like."

"No! Screw that! It's you who can't see the big picture! You've allowed those fucking dragons to turn your head and now you can't think for yourself. I know about your precious Soulbound. Binding your soul to a dragon. Gods!" He slammed a fist into the wall and Sera yelped as plaster trickled down. Kaesus stared at the wall for a moment before his shoulders slumped forward in defeat.

He buried his face in his hands and kept his body turned away from her.

Sera sucked in a rattling breath when she realised she'd been holding it during his tirade. Her skin prickled from the adrenaline racing through her body. All she wanted to do was leap from the bed and run away. But with her ankles and wrists tied down, it was impossible.

"I'm sorry." The words were mumbled and Kaesus kept his head down. "I shouldn't have lost my temper."

Sera stared incredulously as the man who called himself her father took a shuddering breath. *He just said sorry. I never thought I'd hear those words come out of his mouth.* He raised his chin and met her gaze. His irises had warmed to a hue similar to hers. More sapphire than ice. She frowned at the sudden change.

He cracked his neck and ran his fingers through his hair, a habit he seemed to perform under stress. "I came in here because I wanted to explain some of my actions to you. I had hoped that if you could understand why I did what I did, maybe you'd be able to find a way to accept me as your father." He cast a rueful look at the damaged wall. "I'm afraid I'm not doing a very good job of connecting with you. When I saw that look of fear on your face, I just... lost it."

Sera stared at him, not quite sure what to say.

"Will you forgive my bad behaviour, Sera? Will you allow me to speak my piece?"

She hesitated before nodding mutely and waited for him to begin.

He perched on the end of her bed and crossed one of his legs over the other. Brushing an invisible piece of lint off his trousers, he told her everything. "I've been blessed with a long life," he began. "I freely admit that it has been due to the magic of mythics. I offered myself as a guinea pig for the Alchemists to find ways to extend our lives and reduce disease. The trials have had some great success. However, I do sometimes wonder if there are some side effects not measured on their tests..." he trailed off and stared blankly at the wall for a moment. Shaking his head as if to clear it of unwelcome thoughts, he continued, "The Mythic War was gruesome. There was so much death on both sides. I was there when Hunter Ajax came back and told us his story. Of how he found Tracker Borin and the Sapphire Dragon. How she'd hypnotised Borin into protecting her. How she'd killed him when Ajax tried to turn him against her. So, Ajax killed her. He brought her wings back as proof. I took one of her feathers as a keepsake. We had no idea that the death of one of their own would stir the dragons into such a frenzy." He paused and chewed on his lip. "I didn't mean to turn this into a history lesson, sorry. All that was the lead up to tell you that that feather in your room was from me. It belonged to the Sapphire Dragon. I was wanting you to know that I knew about your connection with the Little Birds. I wanted to see if you were clever enough to figure out my plan. But maybe that wasn't fair of me. I didn't know what you were like." He cocked his head as he assessed her. "You are smart, but not conniving. You inspire loyalty in your followers and are kind. Perhaps a little too much so for my taste." He shrugged. "When I found out that you were my daughter, I was understandably shocked. Then I became angry, especially after finding out about your connection with those... creatures." He took a steadying breath. "After I had time to digest the information, I decided I needed to meet you properly. But once the Director told me of his suspicions that your memories had returned, I knew you wouldn't accept a simple invitation. Which led to my plan of poisoning Allen. Don't worry,"

Kaesus held up his hands in surrender at Sera's venomous expression, "there is no lasting damage. He is strong. The toxin is already working its way out of his system. He will fully recover in no time. When he was ill enough to warrant going to the infirmary, Quill took him from his apartment and brought him here. I knew it was only a matter of time before you went to the infirmary to check on him. At which point you would be told he'd never arrived. Leaving you desperate and open to accepting Frank's help. He would give you the IRC plans that he'd 'stolen,'" he made air quotes with his fingers, "from me, which led us to this moment. You played into my hand beautifully. Initially, I was disappointed. I wanted you to beat me at my own game. But then, you are more like your mother than me. And I fell in love with Elisabeth for those same reasons."

Stepping away from the bed, Kaesus rubbed the back of his neck. He seemed fatigued after his monologue.

Sera opened her mouth and closed it. She cleared her throat and tried again. "That's... twisted."

"I understand how you would think so. But it was the only way I could talk to you. And I made sure that no one you love was killed."

"What about Tormund?" She stared at him accusingly.

"Tormund?"

"The hippogryph the guards killed."

"That was a terrible accident. He was simply in the wrong place at the wrong time. But, the guards were in their rights to use lethal force. He was an escaped prisoner. And they had received no express instructions from myself to keep him alive." He stood and made his way to the head of her bed. Leaning over her, he captured her gaze and held it. "You see, Sera, I can protect you. I can keep your loved ones safe. If you'd only let me be part of your life."

She closed her eyes, holding back tears, and broke the manic gaze of her father.

"I realise it's a lot to take in," he murmured. "I'll leave you to process and I'll send the nurse in to take care of your needs. I'll visit again soon." He pressed his lips briefly to her forehead and exited the room, leaving Sera in a whirlpool of emotions.

# CHAPTER FOUR

"I'M GOING TO INTRODUCE you properly today," Kaesus said the following day, steepling his fingers as he watched her closely. "I have warred with myself as to whether or not it's too soon, but I think it's time."

"Time for what?" Sera demanded, her voice raspy from disuse overnight. She cleared her throat and shifted uncomfortably on the bed. Her ribs still ached from where the squabs had beaten her but they were healing much faster than she expected.

"I want you to understand me, so that you can come to love me—" he held his palms up in a placating gesture in response to her grimace "—in your own time. I know you think I don't deserve your affection, but I believe I can change your mind, if only you can understand my reasoning."

He stood and opened the door, allowing the nurse to push a hoverchair into the room. Sera's forehead crinkled in surprise. The nurse moved quickly, undoing the drip attached to Sera's cannula and monitoring equipment. While she watched the nurse, Kaesus leaned over her body and quickly waved his PSB over each of the cuffs. Before she had a chance to react, he slid an arm under her back and legs, lifting her and placing her gently in the chair. Even with his gentle touch, pain rippled through her torso. The unexpected jolt of pain and shock of the moment froze her brain and she didn't think to run.

Before she knew what was happening, he'd snapped her wrists back into cuffs attached to the chair's arms. She heaved a frustrated sigh and hung her head in defeat. Unlocking the door, Kaesus pushed her into the corridor. The sensation of floating a few centimetres above the floor was foreign, making Sera grip the chair's arms as she waited to grow accustomed to the strange movement. The bright lights of the hallway hurt her eyes but she squinted and counted the doors they passed. From what she could tell, there were six cells per side and one at the end. Three guards stood at regular intervals in the corridor and watched their progress silently. Kaesus pushed her chair to the end door. She froze up. It was the same door he'd dragged her paralysed body through when she'd first arrived here. Passing his PSB over the keypad, he then shifted his body in front of it in order to input a passcode. He stepped back and together they waited for the click. Sera's heart raced as she prepared herself to finally meet her mother.

Once inside the cell, Kaesus clicked a button on the back of Sera's hoverchair, causing it to drop unceremoniously to the ground. She gasped in pain as the abrupt movement jarred her ribs.

*Not completely healed, just yet.*

He stalked to the opposite side of the room to the metal chair where Elisabeth sat, hiding her from view and fiddled with something on her arm.

Straightening, he slipped something into his pocket and turned around with a benign smile. Still hiding Elisabeth from Sera's gaze, he announced, "As a token of my goodwill I am going to leave you both alone to catch up. I realise that it has been many years and you'll have some questions for your mother. I'll just be outside the door if you need anything."

Sera kept her eyes down as she dissected his sentence while the President exited the room. On the surface his words suggested concern for their fragile relationship but she knew they were just a subtle warning that he'd be listening. Scanning the room, she told herself she was searching for any other threats or escape routes, when in reality, she was avoiding looking at the woman in front of her. The shame of knowing she'd been imprisoned here for decades without any help from her daughter was overwhelming. The same white stark walls and lack of decoration greeted Sera as in her own room. The bed had been pushed against the side of the room to allow space for both of their chairs. She finished her perusal and glanced down at her fingers as they tapped a nonsensical tune on the chair arm.

*What do you say to the woman you thought was dead for over twenty years?*

"Seraphina." The voice was scratchy yet gentle and dragged her gaze up.

Sera finally met her mother's eyes and twisted her lips up into a half smile. Half a dozen greetings flitted through her mind, all of them seeming idiotic. To break the silence, eventually, she said, "Hey."

*Was that anti-climactic? Yeah, but what else am I supposed to say?*

Elisabeth sat in a simple metal chair, also shackled. Sera's eyes travelled over her mother's body. She was extraordinarily skinny with no muscle tone. Her eyes flicked down to the cannula in her wrist, where bruising spread out around the needle. The subtle scent of sandalwood teased Sera's senses. Her red hair hung limply against her head. Yet her blue eyes filled with warmth when she smiled at Sera.

*How in the Four Gods' names can she still smile after being stuck in here for so long?*

"It's so good to see you," said Elisabeth.

Working her jaw, Sera struggled to find the right words. She finally blurted out, "I thought you were dead."

Elisabeth dropped her eyes, ashamed.

*What does she need to be ashamed about? She's the victim here.*

"I'm so sorry, Sera," she whispered. "I should have been there for you growing up. I feel like a terrible mother. My only recompense was that Mal didn't know that you were his. I had hoped that, by being a good little prisoner, he would be happy. I hoped he'd never find out about you. But now, even that saving grace has been lost."

Sera frowned. "It's not your fault. It's not like you had a choice." She jerked her head toward the door and whispered, "He's the deranged one who uses abduction like a currency."

Her mother gave a wry smile. "You're right there." Her eyes traced Sera's face, drinking her in. "I can't quite believe you're here. You're all grown up," she choked out. "I was so happy when you were born. So very happy. And then Mal," she spat the name, "took it all away." She leaned her face onto her shoulder to wipe away the tears spilling from her eyes, unable to use her hands due to the restraints. "I didn't dare tell him you were his child. I thought that I could keep you safe. But if I'd known he was going to find out about you despite my efforts, I would have... I could have—" Elisabeth broke off with an anguished cry.

"You could have done nothing and most likely we all would have been captured or killed that much sooner," Sera pointed out.

"I thought it would be better this way," she said, "but I am so sorry for the grief I caused you and Allen."

"Have you seen Dad?" Sera asked.

Elisabeth's brow knitted together and she hesitated before asking, "You mean Allen, right?

Sera snorted derisively. "Of course I mean Allen. That man out there," she scrunched up her nose, "is not my father."

"Wait!" Elisabeth's eyes rounded in horror. "Do you mean to say Allen is here? Mal captured him too?"

Sera cringed. "Yes. We didn't know what was happening at the time but Kaesus poisoned Dad. When I went to the MRO's infirmary to check on him, I found out he wasn't there. He'd already been brought here but I didn't know that. Turns out Kaesus wanted me to go to the MRO so Frank, the AI, could offer his help and I'd be desperate enough to accept it. He fed me the plans to the IRC so I would fall into his trap." She gave a heavy sigh. "Which I stupidly fell for. And now, because of me, my old teacher is dead, my dad is captured and my Soulbound is stuck in a coma."

"Your... Soulbound?" Elisabeth whispered the words hesitantly.

"Oh. Right. I forgot that you don't know anything. Erm... where to start?" She briefly filled in her mother on the events that had transpired since Arius abducted her. She finished her monologue with, "Everything was looking peachy, until Kaesus stole Dad. Now, the three of us are stuck in here."

Her mother stared at her, eyes shining with some unspoken emotion. Eventually she asked, "This Arius fellow. Is he good to you? Just because you're Soulbound doesn't mean he can disrespect you." She frowned sternly.

"Hold up for one minute. Out of all of that, you're asking about the healthiness of my relationship? The fact that dragons are still alive and I have some weird mystical connection with one of them doesn't bother you?"

Elisabeth blushed and ducked her head.

"Which means that you knew dragons weren't extinct?"

"I'm sorry. I can't explain how I know. Your grandmother made me swear an oath."

"Huh. So, you're under the same oath as her? Oh, by the way, I found out that Del is my Nanna. Dad was a bit put out that you never told him."

Elisabeth strained against her bonds in agitation.

"I'm sorry," Sera said quickly. "I didn't think about how that would sound when it came out of my mouth. I didn't mean to accuse you of anything. It's just been... really weird. For all of us. There have been so many facets of my life that I took for granted. And now I've found out I've been living in a lie."

"It's not been fair on you," murmured Elisabeth gently. "I'm the one who should be sorry. I wish I could tell you everything. But the truth is, I don't know all of our family's secrets either. For those few that I do know, I've been bound to silence. If you ever find out for yourself, my oath will be lifted."

"It's okay. Please don't apologise. We can only do what we think is right at any one moment in time. You couldn't have known how this would play out."

"I should have had a better idea than I did," Elisabeth grumbled.

Sera cocked her head, confused, until realisation dawned. "I saw a vision in a Seeing Pool. Of you and... Malcolm," she said the name through gritted teeth, "talking. You told him you'd had a vision. That you had seen you'd have a baby together. A baby named Seraphina."

Her mother sucked in a breath and whispered, "Yes. I remember that. I have the ability to See but my visions slowed down after I gave birth to you. I broke off my relationship with Mal shortly after that." She paused and rubbed her thumb against her fisted fingers, seeming to struggle with her words. "After I ended things, I saw Mal one more time. I knew it was a bad idea. I knew I wouldn't be able to resist him. And it was then that I conceived you."

No censure clouded Sera's gaze as she watched her mother wrestle with the story. She only wished she could reach over and wipe away her tears.

Elisabeth raised her chin defiantly. "I don't regret it though. If I hadn't gone back for that one night, I would never have had you. And you were my world. You are my world."

"How did that work, timing wise? I mean, I've never had kids, but I know it takes nine months. How did you get away with falling pregnant to Malcolm and convincing Allen that I was his?"

"Allen and I had been friends for years and he was always there for me. But I'd been so caught up in Mal's charm that I never gave Allen the time of day. Once the blinkers were off, I realised what a special man he was. He'd been in love with me for years so it was an easy relationship to fall straight into after I broke things off with Mal." She gave Sera a fierce look and said, "I want you to know that, while my relationship with your stepfather may have started out partly due to convenience, I grew to love him deeply. The slow kind of love that can stand the test of time.

"Allen desperately wanted a family, so when I realised I was pregnant to Mal, I... lied." She dropped her gaze. "We'd only been together a few weeks when I took a pregnancy test. I simply moved our due date by a month and said you arrived early. Allen was ecstatic when I told him we were expecting. We were married within two months and the sweet man insisted he take my name, since I'd told him I had no family. Lying to him... it was one of the hardest things I've ever done. It felt so wrong but it was the only way I knew to protect you. If Mal knew that you were his... well. Now, he does, and look where that's landed you." She sniffed and awkwardly wiped her face on her shirt again.

"I wish I could give you a hug," Sera whispered.

Elisabeth shot her a watery smile. "I do too, precious girl."

"Thank you for sharing that with me," she added.

"Again, I'm so sorry. I've made some terrible choices in my life. Ones I hope you never have to make. I hope you can forgive me."

"Already forgiven, Mum."

Elisabeth beamed through her tears but folded in on herself when the door opened behind Sera.

"Okay, my girls, I think that's enough catching up for one day." Kaesus clicked the button again on the back of Sera's chair and it whirred to life, hovering a few centimetres above the floor. He turned her around and pushed her out of the cell. Leaning over the side, she looked back and threw a quick smile at her mother as she disappeared behind the door.

*I have to get her out of here.*

# CHAPTER FIVE

IN SILENCE, KAESUS PUSHED her chair down the hall, back towards her door, passing the three taciturn guards.

Sera broke the peace with a question. "Why did you take my mother away?"

"It's complicated. You wouldn't understand."

"Try me."

"Some mysteries were meant to stay that way."

"Fine then. Keep your secrets. Answer me this, instead. Why do you hate dragons?"

"I don't hate them," he said, bristling.

"Sure seems like it," she replied. "You were a part of the movement that wiped them out and when you became President, you forbade anyone to talk about them."

"Dragons have been very useful to me. I respect their power. I appreciate their talents. But they don't fit in the world I want to build. So, they had to be eliminated."

"The world where you rule everyone?"

He stopped walking and a heavy pause sat between them.

"You still don't understand," he growled. "You need to understand the big picture. If I hadn't taken control, Mandar City would have fallen into ruin. When I took over the Presidency after the Mythic War, I made the decision to restrict the masses from talking about dragons. We didn't need a civil war while we were still recovering from the Mythic War. If I had let conversations about dragons run, idle chatter would have turned into conspiracy theories that would have turned into a banner for a portion of the population to rally behind. Citizens would have fought amongst themselves and we were already hurting too much. Why do you think I focused only on rebuilding shelters and the farming industry? I paid the media to keep the dialogue focussed on the lack of homes and food so I could maintain control of the masses. I had to stop the threat of infighting. I didn't bother allocating funds to the transport industry for a reason. If I'd allowed people to travel outside the country and freely speak about what was happening here, outsiders would have fanned the flames of unrest. This way, everyone stayed in their bubble, everyone grew comfortable and this became their new normal." Malcolm knelt in front of Sera and stared earnestly into her eyes. "I did what I had to do to save the people of Mandar City."

She stared back at him, her eyebrows drawn together, conflicted. *It makes a twisted kind of sense.* She suddenly realised his skin wasn't nearly as lined as it had been yesterday. "What happened to your face?" she challenged him.

He touched his cheeks, confused, and asked, "What do you mean?"

"Your..." she cast about for the right word, "wrinkles. I noticed how much you'd aged yesterday. But now... you look... younger."

He pushed up from the ground and turned his face away, subconsciously fingering something in his pocket. "I told you. I've been blessed with a long life thanks to the magic of mythics."

"Yeah, but that was such a big change—"

"Don't worry about it," he interrupted her.

She opened her mouth to argue but shut it again when an Alchemist rushed in, clearly identified by her white uniform, pushing a trolley in front of her.

"President Kaesus, sir! You asked me to come see you if I had an update on Exhibit 376! I've just discovered the most fascinating thing-" She skidded to a stop when Kaesus held his hand up to stop her verbal barrage. When the Alchemist halted her headlong sprint, something fell off her table. Sera frowned as she tried to make out the muddled pile of hard objects on the sterile medical trolley.

"Not now."

"But, Sir! When we removed the nerves that line the interior of the exoskelet—"

"I said, not now!" he snarled at the woman. "If you want to keep your job, you will leave immediately. I will come down to the lab later tonight. Go."

She dashed forward and picked up the thing that had fallen in front of Sera's chair, keeping her eyes on the floor. Sera watched as the Alchemist nervously placed the bony item back on the table with shaking hands and fled the hallway.

Realisation dawned and Sera spoke slowly, "Was that?" She paused, goosebumps coating her skin. "It couldn't be." She glanced up at Kaesus, her eyes swimming with unshed tears of anger. "Was that the body of the scorpius I captured a couple of months ago? It's been mutilated." Her voice broke over the last word.

His face blank, Kaesus crossed his arms defensively. "I don't know," he muttered, refusing to meet her accusatory glare. "I don't keep track of every mythic that's brought in."

"Why would you do that?" she demanded. "Scorpius aren't good or bad. You can't label them as rogue and condemn them to death! They simply do what they need to do to survive. When I called that scorpius attack in, I thought the IRC would simply hold the mythic in a safe containment unit while the MRO took some measurements and notes before releasing it back to the wild. I would never have called it in if I'd known it would be killed! And, not only killed, but literally cracked open and pulled to pieces." She retched.

"Look," Kaesus said and placed his hand on her shoulder, squeezing it reassuringly. "I know it's hard to understand right now but every creature has its purpose. That scorpius wasn't killed for no reason. Its chitin will be used to assist our armourers improve the protective suits of our Hunters. Its flesh has been fed to the carnivorous prisoners. Its blood and innards are used by our dedicated Alchemists to create remedies that will improve our quality of life. There is no waste here. There is a purpose to every death. I don't expect you to understand yet. But I hope that one day, with enough time, you will."

Sera's heart twisted at his words. While she understood the need to hunt and not to waste any part of the animal's body, she couldn't condone it on a massive scale. Especially when it was being done in secret. She asked him as much, "Surely, it's illegal not to tell the Trackers and Hunters that most of the rogue mythics they catch are used for spare parts? Why do the MRO even have the slogan of 'Capture, don't kill'?" She answered herself immediately. "Because some of the mythics need to be kept alive so the Alchemists can use their bodies while their organs are still fresh." Her stomach roiled, threatening to empty itself on the linoleum.

Kaesus said nothing, and simply continued to push her chair toward the cell.

Aaron appeared in front of them then, guiding another trolley laden with food toward her door. The nurse followed him silently, ready to hook Sera back up to the vitals monitor. Aaron smiled benignly and waited for them to enter before both he and the nurse followed them inside. The room suddenly felt very crowded. Kaesus didn't greet Aaron, instead focussing on moving Sera back to her bed and shackling her to it once again. The nurse helped hold her, dissuading any plans of escape she might have entertained. Once the nurse had replenished the bag of fluids hanging on the rod and hooked her cannula back onto the drip, Kaesus' scent wafted over Sera once again. This time he smelt vaguely of sandalwood.

He straightened and said, "I hope you reflect long and hard on our discussions from today. Remove your emotions from the equation and think about it logically. Everything I do is for the people."

*Exactly. For the* people. *Not the mythics.* But she kept her mouth shut and exhaled noisily once he'd disappeared. She turned her head to Aaron but pulled up short when she saw the thunderous look on his face.

"I heard what he said about the scorpius, Sera. I had no idea."

She'd never seen the Negotiator this angry.

"What's the point of my job if they're just going to use the mythics' bodies for science? Why keep up the charade after all these years? All my life, I have worked hard to learn the cultures of the various species of mythics. I learnt so I could help them. I could argue on their behalf, I could teach them our ways so they didn't make the same mistake twice. Some of the mythics under my care were released with warnings, sure. But most of them were left in the IRC until their trial. And all this time I thought it was my fault!" He pounded a fist against the serving area of the trolley, making the plates jump. Sera flinched at the clattering. "I thought I wasn't a good enough Negotiator to get them home. But now I find out that they've been harvesting them all this time? What the actual fuck?"

"That's why I need to save them, Aaron. I need to get out of here with my family and fix this," she pleaded.

He clasped his hands together and let out a loud exhale. Once again, he fixed her pillow in order to place his mouth near her ear and whispered, "I'll help you, Sera. I had an idea about getting your dragon unhooked. I'll put my plan into action right away."

"What are you going to do?"

"I won't tell you the details. That way, if I'm caught out, you can claim ignorance without having to try and lie." He grinned at her. "No offence, but from what I've seen, you're a terrible liar." Squeezing her shoulder gently, he said, "I don't have a plan yet on how to get you all out since I only have access to your cell. But, don't worry. We'll figure this out."

# CHAPTER SIX

SERA SLEPT FITFULLY THAT night. Dreams clouded her mind and wouldn't allow her a restful slumber.

While she dreamt of blue feathers she heard a voice whispering, "I'm sorry."

The voice was foreign with both high and low tones. Yet, she felt as if she'd heard it before.

"I'm so sorry, Seraphina," the voice came again, tugging her out of her dream.

Disorientated, she opened her eyes to the pitch-black room. The eerie silence struck her; someone had turned her vitals monitor off.

The voice came again, this time to her right. "Please, don't be afraid. I just wanted to say I'm sorry."

She screamed and tried to jerk away, forgetting for a moment that she was still imprisoned. The shackles held her down and her eyes scanned the darkness frantically, desperately trying to find some hint of the stranger. Her heart beat loudly in her ears and her breath came in short pants. A flicker of a shadow stirred in the corner and red eyes flashed for a moment before being enveloped in darkness once again.

"I mean you no harm," came the stranger's voice again.

"Who are you?" she demanded.

"My name is Quill," they replied.

"You're Quill?" she screeched. "You're the one who—"

Sera choked on her words, suddenly feeling like she couldn't breathe through a suffocating cloud of smoke.

"Hush. Yes, it's my fault that you're here. Please, don't scream. I swear, I wish you no ill will." Quill released her before drifting to the other side of her bed.

Her eyes flicked up toward the corner of the ceiling where the camera should be. No red light met her examination, making her frown. "What's happened to the camera?"

"I disabled it," Quill said matter-of-factly. Turning her vitals monitor back on, the mythic floated into the machine's faint glow. The being was a creature seemingly made up of pulsing black smoke.

Sera narrowed her eyes. "You're a shadow."

"You are correct. So, you have seen my kind before then?" they asked.

"Yes," she replied. "Years ago, I watched a trial at the courthouse where they had a shadow convicted of murder."

The shadow's form crumpled in on itself and its multi-toned voice turned bitter. "That was my parent, Inca Soleque. The judge falsely convicted them of Hector's murder in order to capture both them and myself. We are skilled at concealing ourselves so the President likes to use us as his little spies. He still holds my parent prisoner so I follow his orders."

Horrified at finding out the new way the President abused mythics, Sera struggled to work through the many questions she had. She focussed on the simplest one and asked, "Why do you call them your parent? Was it your mother or your father?"

"We are a species of hermaphrodites," Quill explained. "We only have one parent since we are comprised of both female and male genders." Their smoky edges flurried in agitation. "While you've been trapped here, I've been watching and listening, and have learnt a great deal. I wanted you to know that I greatly regret my role in bringing you here. Whilst you never saw me," the voice deepened to only one tone, the same voice she'd heard over the phone, "you spoke to me when I hacked the MRO's phone system. The President told me I had to convince you that your father was in the infirmary but that you wouldn't be able to see him until the morning. He wanted to see what you would do. He threatened to murder my family if I didn't follow orders. But now, I've had enough." The shadow grew larger in stature, the smoky tendrils pulsing. "I want to help you. Following orders hasn't released my family, but fighting back might help save someone else's. I'm going to get you out of here, Seraphina."

"Last time I believed someone wanted to double-cross the President, it turned out to be a trap. Do you think I'm naïve enough to fall for the same trick twice?" she scoffed.

The shadow gave a sad little sigh. "I can't say I'm surprised by your reaction. I swear my intentions are honourable. If I release you right now, would that make you trust me? That way you know I haven't had time to inform anyone of my plans."

She eyed the shadow doubtfully. "I'm sorry, but I don't think I can. This could all be a setup. Kaesus could be waiting right outside the door to capture me again. And anyway, I can't leave without my family." She smiled sadly. "My mother, my father and my Soulbound are all trapped here too."

"Then I will free them as well," Quill proclaimed.

"How?" Sera asked, not daring to fan the embers of hope in her heart.

"Like this," they said and pushed a shadowy tendril into the inner mechanism of the handcuff that ensnared her left wrist. It popped open, making Sera gasp. Quill continued on with the other three manacles, each opening with a snap. She sat up, rubbing her wrists where the metal had chafed the skin.

"I will go now and release your family from their bonds, one at a time. Once you are all free, I will unlock your doors so that no one is left alone in the hallway. Get ready to fight your way out of here."

Sera watched incredulously as the shadow floated up to the ceiling and condensed into wisps of smoke, filtering into the vent. She pushed herself out of bed, surprised to find the pain in her ribs was almost gone. Moving quickly, she disconnected the heart rate and blood pressure monitors. Bending down, she rummaged through the cabinet beneath the table, eventually finding a plaster. Lastly, with some difficulty, she pulled the cannula out of her arm, keeping pressure on her elbow while she quickly applied the plaster to stop the bleeding. She stretched, thankful that whatever the President had given her through the drip had sped up the recovery of her ribs. She stared around the empty room, not knowing what to think. The logical side of her brain refused to accept that she was receiving help from the mythic who had tricked her into thinking her father was going to the infirmary. But her heart remained hopeful that it was possible for people, or in this case, mythics, to change and learn from their mistakes. She could only hope this was the case with Quill.

A sensible idea suddenly popped into her head. *Why didn't I think of this sooner?* She opened her mind and followed Quill's path through the vents. The shadow had a soft orange aura, almost like the glow of a sunset. Quill entered the vent in her mother's room and paused beside the bed. A short time later, Elisabeth's aura moved off the bed. Sera crowed aloud in delight but quickly clapped her hands over her mouth. *No need to alert the squabs just yet.*

Abandoning Quill and Elisabeth, she sent her mind in the other direction, seeking her Soulbound. Tickling the edges of his consciousness, she sensed that his mind felt different from her earlier attempts to connect with him. She felt him startle awake.

*Arius? Can you hear me?*

*Seraphina? Are you all right?*

*I'm fine! What about you? I haven't been able to connect with you for days!*

*Thank the Gods you're safe! Yes, I am as well as can be expected. Still feeling a little groggy from whatever they injected me with but it seems to be wearing off.*

She quickly filled Arius in on everything that had happened whilst he had been unconscious and shared her fears that Quill would trick them again.

He comforted her by saying, *Don't worry. If the shadow tries to mess with you again, I'll eat him. Oh, Quill has arrived now. I'll let you know how we go on the eating front.*

There was an anxious pause whilst Arius conversed aloud with the shadow. His aura remained calm, allowing Sera some comfort while she waited for his verdict.

*Quill just came through the vent in my ceiling and took out the sentry who was standing guard at my door. He's releasing me from my restraints now. The shadow is genuine, I'm sure of it. See you soon, sweet Seraphina. I cannot wait to hold you in my arms once more.*

# CHAPTER SEVEN

HOPPING FROM ONE FOOT to the other, Sera waited impatiently for Quill to return. Yet, when her cell door finally opened, she had to bite back a yelp of surprise.

Quill chuckled, the smoke pulsing in time with his mirth. "Come." A tendril separated from the main body of smoke and beckoned her forward. "It is time to be reunited with your family."

The shadow disappeared and the sound of another door unlocking made Sera grin. She hurried to the doorway of her cell and cautiously peered into the hallway. The bright lights made her feel terribly exposed, but the sight of two lifeless guards on the floor eased her apprehension. There was no sign of any other squabs but Quill dragged the bodies inside her cell to avoid raising the alarm prematurely. While she held her door open for Quill, someone cleared their throat, making her head snap around. On the opposite side of the corridor and to her left stood Arius, his eyes running over her body, drinking in the sight of her. In return, she examined his body for obvious injuries and took in the unflattering boxy gown they had him in.

"Don't I look good?" he asked sardonically.

"You'd look good in anything," she said before throwing herself into his arms. Their lips met in a tender kiss and she wrapped her arms around his torso.

They broke their kiss and he tucked her head under his chin before murmuring into her hair, "You don't know how good it feels to have you in my arms again."

"I think I have a fair idea," she argued playfully.

His chest heaved in silent laughter. She breathed him in, relishing the indescribable scent of comfort and warmth. She felt the moment that he froze, then he gripped the tops of her arms and turned her around. Her heart felt as if it were breaking and healing in that single moment as she watched her father and mother come face-to-face after more than two decades apart.

"Elisabeth? This isn't possible..." Allen croaked as he stared at his wife in disbelief.

"My darling," she cried in response and held her skinny arms up.

He stumbled forward and fell into her embrace.

Arius squeezed Sera's hand. They waited silently while Sera's parents reconnected.

Quill drifted forward. "I hate to ruin the moment but we best keep moving."

Sera nodded and released Arius' hand before stepping forward. "This is it," she said with a fervent tone. "Tonight is the night we escape." She gripped her parents on the shoulders and gave them a reassuring squeeze. She grimaced when she noticed the tears in her father's Tracker uniform, where cuts showed through the fabric from the guards' abuse. His face was bruised and swollen and some of the wounds on his arms were weeping. Allen hadn't been cared for nearly as well as Sera had during his imprisonment in the IRC. "We have friends on the outside that can help us. We're not alone in this." She paused and ran her eyes over her mother's skeletal frame. "I know you're both hurt, and I want you to stay safe. Stick with Arius and we'll try to sneak out. We won't go through the service tunnel this time; the President tricked me into coming in that way which means he'll be watching it." She ran her hands over her head anxiously. "I don't know how else to get out without raising the alarm. Any ideas?"

Arius queried, "What type of boundary does this prison have? I was unconscious when they brought me here so I never saw it."

Sera shrugged. "As far as I know, it's an electrified fence. It's in the shape of a dome that goes over the entire IRC. It was purpose-built to keep flighted mythics from escaping when they're let out for exercise." Allen nodded in agreement whilst keeping Elisabeth tucked close against his side.

Arius tapped his chin thoughtfully. "Well, what if we head straight to the boundary fence and I can make a hole for us to escape through?"

"How exactly do you plan on doing that? The entire thing is electrified. If any of us touch it, we'll be fried," Allen asked, raising an eyebrow.

Sera blew a breath out through her teeth. "I keep forgetting how little you know, Dad. Don't freak out, but Arius is a dragon. He'll transform once we're out of the building and throw a fireball or something," she said it light-heartedly but studied her father's face, waiting for his reaction.

Allen's eyes bugged for a moment but he quickly schooled his features into a neutral expression. "Well... That should save us some time."

She smiled at his ready acceptance and glanced at her Soulbound. Arius didn't touch her but the look of love in his gaze filled her with heat and passion. And Sera knew she'd give everything she had to get them all out alive.

She brushed his mind tenderly and whispered, *I love you.*

*I am yours,* he rumbled back, *forever and always. I will do everything I can to protect the ones you love.*

Aloud she said to them, "Let's go."

Allen grabbed Sera's arm, forcing her to stop. He studied her intensely and asked, "Are you sure this is the best option?" His brows lowered in a pained expression. "I... I need to keep you and your mother safe. I can't lose either of you. Not again."

"Honestly, Dad? I don't know. But I don't have any other ideas. The longer we stay here, the more likely it is that we'll be captured again. We need to leave now."

A small smile passed over Allen's lips and he released her with a nod of approval. He murmured, "That's my girl. You're right."

She grinned at him. "You taught me well."

Quill moved to the head of the group. "Stay quiet now. There should only be two guards on duty and the President is supposed to be in a meeting tonight. However, he has laid false trails in the past so you can never fully trust what his itinerary says. We'll sneak while we can, but be prepared to kill on sight," Quill whispered. "By the way, Sera, I believe this is yours." The shadow plucked an object from within their smoky form and held it out.

Sera cried out joyfully at the sight of Firinne in its sheath. She gripped the staghorn handle in relief, thankful to have her blade returned, then abruptly shot her mother a look when an unexpected thought popped into her head. "Mum," she asked hesitantly, "Did you want to use Firinne? It was yours after all."

"No, darling," her mother said. "I'll be flat out walking anywhere, let alone fighting. It's been your blade for a long time now, you keep it, my girl. Use it well."

With a nod of understanding, she turned back to Quill. "I can't tell you how much this means to me. I'm so grateful."

The smoky tendrils swirled in before Quill added, "I found your PSB in the same box but decided to leave it. I wouldn't put it past the President to try and track it once you've escaped."

"Smart thinking," she replied. Then, taking a deep breath, Sera cast her mind forward and sensed the two guards Quill had mentioned. They were standing outside the front doors of the high-security block. One turned toward the entry and Sera hissed, "Incoming!" before quickly flattening herself into a cell doorway. Allen shot her a look of confusion before grabbing Elisabeth and following suit, bracing a protective arm in front of his wife, keeping his body in front of hers.

*Oops, I'll have to tell Dad about my talent. But maybe later.* She glanced across the hall at Arius who was trying to conceal his frame in the narrow space. *Not the best hiding place but better than milling around in the corridor.*

The main door opened and the squab began making his way down the hall, yawning as he marched. Sera heard the door automatically hiss shut behind him. Her muscles coiled, ready to spring into an attack. Her mouth twisted at the idea of killing a human again. Arius noticed her grimace and leapt before she could, grabbing the man by the throat and smashing him into the wall. His head made a loud bang as it hit the plaster and she winced at the noise. The guard slid to the floor, either unconscious or dead, she couldn't tell.

The door hissed open again and the second guard strode briskly through, calling out as she came, "What was that, Baxter?" As her eyes fell on the body in the middle of the hall, she shrieked.

Arius was already sprinting towards her as she began to call for backup, shouting hastily into her wristband. He tackled her to the ground and incapacitated her quickly. The buzz of a squab responding to her call for assistance crackled from her PSB.

"Well, shit," said Allen with a wry twist of his lips. "Guess it's time to go out with all guns blazing." He retrieved two pistols from the inert guards and counted the bullets left in the magazines before handing one to Elisabeth. "We've got this, hun," he said and gave her a kiss on the cheek. "I won't let anything happen to you."

She blushed like a school girl and Sera's heart squeezed to see her parents rekindling their love.

Quill flitted to the head of their party and said, "Get ready."

The shadow sent tendrils of black smoke snaking into the keypad beside the door the guards had just rushed through. The light above the screen flashed green and the doors slid open.

*The biggest hurdle is down. Now we just need to get through the IRC's boundary and we'll be free. Here's hoping the Gods are on our side.*

The five of them dashed out the door and turned left, while Sera thanked the Gods for an overcast evening. They followed the wall of the cell block, turning left again once they reached its corner. Keeping the main IRC building at their back as they headed straight towards the boundary fence, they concealed themselves in the shadows as best they could, using the building for cover. Quill proved their usefulness by floating to the roof of the cellblock and smashing the floodlights, casting them all into darkness.

A voice called from the shadows, "Who goes there?"

They crept along the wall, each praying to the Gods for a miracle.

"If you don't identify yourself, we will be forced to open fire."

They hurried away from the squab and into the open space between the cell block and the boundary. With fifty metres between them and the fence, Arius took the lead of their group while Allen covered the rear, ready to fire. Between the two men, Sera held tightly onto her mother's arm, helping to keep her upright as she stumbled forward. Sera cursed the lack of cover between them and the fence. The domed mesh stretched up over their heads, but all they needed was to make a gap in the wire to sneak through.

A shot rang through the air, whizzing past her right ear. Allen swore.

Glancing over her shoulder, Sera winced as she saw half a dozen shadowy figures sprinting from the main building of the IRC, responding to their comrade's cut-off call for help. As the guards slowed to file through the gate of the fence that divided the two sections of the prison, Allen took aim. He fired his borrowed weapon, taking out three guards in quick succession. As the sound of gunfire echoed through the compound, a high-pitched alarm sounded, and more guards came surging out of their respective cell blocks.

"Fuck a duck," Sera muttered.

Arius shot her a quizzical look at the unfamiliar term. She shook her head, promising to explain later. *If there is a later.*

Her mother stopped and, shaking her arm free of Sera's grip, raised the pistol Allen had given her, holding it steady with two hands. A grim look of satisfaction filled Elisabeth's face as she took out two squabs without hesitation. They weren't clean shots, but the guards went down and stayed down. Return fire peppered the ground around them but, partially concealed as they were by the high-security block they'd just escaped from, the bullets stayed wide of their group. With the mass influx of enemies, all thought of slipping away unnoticed was gone, so Arius shed his human skin, bursting into his dragon form. He stamped his feet and roared a challenge to their enemies, his fangs glinting in the dim light. Pandemonium erupted from the main building as squabs shouted to one another about the escaped dragon.

Sera caught a glimpse of her parents staring at her Soulbound in awe. She interrupted their gawking with a warning. "Be careful! When I originally broke in, some of the guards were invisible." She shrugged at the look of astonishment from Allen. "Don't ask me how. I assume it's magic?" She cast her mind out, touching briefly on the auras of the men and women at their backs who were running to find cover. The five of them were only twenty metres away from the boundary fence when Sera noticed six auras coming from the opposite side of the high-security cell block.

"Six guards incoming from my seven o'clock," she called, "but I'm not sure if they're invisible or not." Suddenly, another life shone brightly in her mind and she gasped, "Idris!"

*Nice to see you're still alive, girl.* It was a comfort to hear his familiar voice in her head.

*Same to you, cat.*

She heard the smile in his voice when he replied. *I deserved that. I see you've got a tagalong.*

She frowned for a moment before realising he meant Elisabeth. *Yes. My mother.*

*Well, well, well. How intriguing. I'd love to hear the whole story later. But let's get you all out of here first. I am sorry for abandoning you when I did. However, I saw how many you were up against and knew we wouldn't win a battle that night. But I figured you could use some extra paws to launch an escape plan. And I couldn't exactly fetch them for you if I were locked up in there with you, could I?*

Peering through the boundary fence, Sera suddenly recognised the shadowy shapes appearing from the forest. The black lynx had brought the Little Birds out to play.

# CHAPTER EIGHT

ARIUS THUNDERED A BATTLE cry before unleashing a torrent of fire on the nearest section of wire. The barrier sparked as the flames met the electric current. The strands of wire glowed brightly as they heated up, not able to withstand the magic of dragonfire. Portions of the fence began melting away, dripping slags of metal onto the ground. It hissed when it hit the dew-encrusted grass and steam rose into the cool night air. Another volley of bullets came their way. Arius paused his attack on the fence to pull the humans in under his belly to take cover behind his legs.

*What are you doing? You can't take that many hits for us!* Sera exclaimed into his mind.

*Standard gunfire doesn't affect my body. It will simply ricochet off my scales. Allow me to keep you and your family safe. You can help me by keeping an eye out for those cursed arrows and that electric net. We might be in trouble then.*

Sera glanced around and realised Quill had disappeared. Before she could ask her parents where he'd gone, another barrage of gunfire assaulted them and she ducked her head, taking shelter behind a foreleg. Arius turned his head with a snarl and unleashed a fireball the size of a yearling unicorn into the closest group of guards. Screams, along with the scent of charred bodies, filled the air as indistinct orders were shouted between the troops filing out of the IRC. They dragged shields out with them and Sera wondered whether they would hold back Arius' flames.

Idris' voice sounded in her head again. *The shadow and I have got your back with that nasty invisible crowd who were trying to launch a sneak attack. There's no more of the invisible lot to worry about for the time being.*

*Thank you!* She peeked out from behind Arius' leg and saw six bodies on the ground between them and the high-security prison, visible now that they were dead. Her heart squeezed painfully at the unnecessary killing but she knew the only way to escape was to meet violence with violence. She would try to find a diplomatic solution in the future, but there was no talking to the squabs in the heat of the moment. Idris and Quill didn't return to the group immediately, creeping around the back of the building instead, both blending in seamlessly with the dark of the night.

Allen cursed again as both he and Elisabeth ran out of ammunition. "This isn't good," he muttered as more guards poured from the IRC to replace those who had already fallen.

"What can we do?" Sera asked her dad quietly.

"Wait and pray," answered her mother, closing her eyes and dropping her head, her right hand over her heart in prayer. "Caelhi will answer our call."

Sera and Allen shared a troubled look. Neither were of the nature to wait for help.

*We're certainly not used to asking a Goddess for assistance. But maybe, with the strength of the Little Birds, we can make it out.*

Peering out from behind Arius' cover, Sera glanced back to the perimeter and was stunned to see it was more than just a few warriors that had come to help. A small host of mythics and humans had gathered just outside the cover of the tree line, weapons and magic at the ready, waiting for the signal to fight for the Little Birds.

Arius snarled in frustration. "Wait a moment," he called urgently to the gathered Little Birds. "There are enchantments inlaid into the perimeter to keep anyone from getting in or out without authority. I can destroy them with my flames, but it will take longer." He sent a concentrated blast of fire at the fence, where it curled against an invisible barrier. As he focused his blaze on the enchantments, the fire licked up the side of the magical wall, burning away a hole in the extra layer of protection. A minute later, Arius announced, "You can get through now, one at a time." He hung his head and sucked in a few deep breaths, already exhausted from the effort. He murmured to Sera, "It's going to take a lot out of me to make the space big enough for my body to fit through."

She stroked his scaly snout and suggested, "Why don't you just shift into a human so we can escape without needing to enlarge the hole? Then you can return to dragon form so we can fly away from here."

He chuckled weakly. "I appreciate your vote of confidence in my power. However, I fear that I am too weak. I'm afraid that, if I transform again, I will die. As much as burning my way through the fence will sap my energy, I am strongest in my natural form. While it will be exhausting, it won't kill me."

She kissed his snout in understanding and said, "You do whatever you need to do to be safe."

He rumbled deep in his chest in response to her affection and added, "You'll have to keep the guards at bay for a lot longer than I'd hoped."

She caressed his scales and said with an encouraging smile, "Lucky we have the Little Birds to help then, huh?"

Now that the hole was large enough, twenty-odd humans, half a dozen unicorns, two hippogryphs, a pack of werewolves and three taurons with metal chest-plates hurried in through the fence, being careful not to touch the wards. They fanned out around Arius, Sera and her parents, offering their protection. Once they were all through, Arius resumed his inferno, only stopping to send fireballs at the closest guards. Sera fed him some of her energy through their bond, knowing how much power he used to maintain consistent dragonfire. Tor smiled at Sera and Arius before flying into the air with Bels close behind him. Constantine lead the wolves and gave her a wink, his tongue lolling out the side of his mouth. Knowing it was selfish to only worry about her friends, she still whimpered when she noticed Balthazar among the unicorns, hoping he would keep himself safe. The buckskin stallion snorted in her direction, offering his reassurances. The chestnut filly, Rella, was there too. The unicorns began weaving a spell together with their horns, each one glowing a bright white as they pulled up a massive ward over the group. The humans came in behind the mythics, wielding an array of long-range weapons. Tracker Helena and another man ran under Arius' belly, straight to Sera and Allen.

Helena nodded a greeting, before doing a double-take at Elisabeth. "Eli? You're not dead then?" Helena wrapped her up in a brief hug. "No time for chit-chat, sorry." She looked at Sera. "We'll hold off the worst of their attack while your dragon widens the hole. The unicorns' ward should keep the worst of the incoming fire from hitting us, while still allowing our outward attack. As soon as the dragon can get himself out, you all need to get as far away from here as fast as you can."

"What about you?" Sera asked.

"Don't worry about us, we've got an escape plan if shit goes down." She glanced around at her team, before opening her jacket to show a small capsule. Sera flinched at the sight of the innocuous grey shell. She'd seen pictures of these mini-bombs in her textbooks at MINATH. They were only called mini for the size of their casing. There was nothing small about their explosion. Helena continued, "I hope we don't need to use it, but the majority of them will survive if I do have to trigger it."

Allen's brows creased in concern for his boss. "Are you sure about this, Helena?"

She gave a wild grin. "I've never been so sure about anything in my life. It's about time I got the chance to avenge Volkuhn. Who, it turns out, was not the last dragon." She raised her eyes to the scaled belly above her head in wonder before shaking her head to refocus. "Now, quit yapping and let's bring the action!" She passed a box of bullets to Allen and Elisabeth, who quickly began reloading their handguns. She zipped up her jacket and unholstered two pistols of her own, handing one to Sera. The three of them knelt and began firing back towards the IRC.

Revealing the man who had stayed hidden behind her.

"Negotiator Aaron!" Sera cried. "What are you doing here?"

"Well, I thought I'd come along to help free you. But it seems like you're doing a pretty good job of that yourself. I don't think you really need me after all. I might just pack up and go home." He grinned cheekily. "Nah, just kidding. I never get the chance to engage in a good old-fashioned firefight. This is as good a chance as any." He pulled out a pistol, holding it awkwardly as he loaded the magazine.

"Have you…" she paused, not wanting to offend her friend, "Have you shot a gun before?"

He grimaced. "Is it that obvious? No, not much," he admitted. "Only had that bit of training during my apprenticeship. But we kind of focussed on talking mythics out of violence. We weren't really encouraged to engage in it." He snorted. "Nice to see your friend in dragon form." He jerked his head toward Arius' belly and blinked rapidly. "He's not intimidating at all."

She gave a quiet chuckle. "He's really very nice, so long as you're nice to him."

"I'll make sure I am," he muttered under his breath. He closed one eye and took aim.

Sera watched, impressed as he felled a squab with his first bullet. *He might be slow and look awkward doing it, but he's a decent shot.* She turned away and began shooting herself, downing two squabs in quick succession. Whilst she fired, she surveyed the battle raging in front of her, trying to make sense of the chaos. Arius had made good progress on the fence and its enchantments but the hole was not yet large enough for him to squeeze through. She sent him more energy to help him finish his work. The electrified boundary fence still arced and flashed in the background but it was dwarfed by the column of flame pouring from Arius' jaws. Even with her power supplementing his, she could sense his reserves beginning to flag from overexerting himself after being imprisoned for too long in his human form. The unicorns' ward appeared to be deflecting the majority of the bullets away, but the squabs had pulled out their arsenal of mythic-specific weaponry and were gearing up to kill any of their unit who ventured beyond the ward. The two hippogryphs were flying over the main building of the IRC, picking off the snipers who had set up on the roof. One of the taurons stood off to the side of Arius, firing bolts from a cross-bow into the enemy's ranks. Meanwhile, the other two half-bull, half-men had abandoned the safety of the ward and were charging headfirst into the clusters of guards, one swinging a giant hammer and the other simply using his horns. Bullets smacked into their armoured bodies but didn't seem to slow them down. The werewolves were attacking any brave squabs that dared to leave the safety of the main building and tearing them apart. Her stomach roiled at the human bodies littering the ground but she reminded herself that these people had allowed mythics to be harvested for parts for years. As she kept scanning the battlefield, her eyes caught on two lumpy shapes laying on the earth, too large to be humans. Her throat closed as she identified them as a unicorn and a werewolf.

*Please don't be Balthazar or Constantine.*

She scanned their group again and breathed a sigh of relief when she located Balthazar still with the herd of unicorns, maintaining the ward. But she couldn't see Constantine. She worried her lip, before casting her mind out. Almost immediately, she pulled it back in. Holstering her gun, she stomped out from under Arius, away from the fighting and toward the fence, where she circled behind the unicorns. Hands on her hips, she exclaimed, "What in the Four Gods' names are you doing here, Wren?"

# CHAPTER NINE

THE SCRAWNY, DARK-HAIRED BOY poked his head out from behind a unicorn's rump then. "Hi, Miss Sera," he smiled shyly.

"You do not get to act cute and get away with this, Wren!" she hissed and grabbed his jacket, hauling him close to her. She kept his body on her left, away from the direction of the incoming bullets. She didn't want to rely solely on the unicorns' magic. Once they were back under Arius' belly, she demanded, "What were you thinking of, coming here?"

He scuffed a tattered shoe in the dirt, not looking at her.

Helena stopped firing and turned to look at them, glowering at the boy. "I told you to stay in the city."

He crossed his arms and glared up at her defiantly. "I want to help, too."

She glared back. "You're a child. This is a battlefield. You cannot be here. It's not safe."

"It's not safe for me on the streets, either." He stuck out a lip petulantly before flicking his eyes to meet Sera's. "I came because I wanted to save Miss Sera."

Sera hugged him fiercely and kissed the top of his head, her messy braid falling into his face and tickling his nose. "You're a sweet kid. But I would never forgive myself if something happened to you." She looked around desperately. "We need to find a way to get you home safely."

"I don't have a home," he mumbled and buried his head into her grey shirt.

She grimaced at her faux pas. "I'm sorry. I meant to say, go back to the Peace Tree. At least there, you won't be getting shot at."

Idris appeared at their side. "I'll take the boy and make sure he gets back safely."

Sera went to lay a hand on his shoulder but pulled it away when she realised his coat was slick with blood that wasn't his. "Thank you. For everything," she said simply, hoping he comprehended the depth of her gratitude.

Idris nudged her gently with his wet nose, then magically flared the black flames that usually lined his neck and spine to cover his entire body, burning away the blood on his coat. Extinguishing his fire completely, he crouched, offering his back to Wren. The boy clambered on and Idris stood.

Wren looked up at Sera with brown eyes that shone. "Promise you'll come see me when you get out?"

"I promise I'll see you again once it's safe."

Hanging off the lynx, Wren hugged her awkwardly around the middle. She squeezed him tightly back.

Idris gave her another nudge. *I don't want to alarm the boy, but you need to know. There are at least fifty guards still fighting and they've called for back-up. Quill is doing further recon and will report to you shortly.*

*Thanks, Idris. Stay safe.*

Arius stopped burning the fence at a mental instruction from Idris. The lynx nodded once and leapt forward, Wren grabbing his neck to avoid falling off and laughing at the sudden movement. They sped away, leaping over the melted wire and vanishing into the night. A blur of black captured Sera's attention from the corner of her eye and she spun around.

Quill appeared, their black tendrils difficult to distinguish from the natural shadows. They slipped along the ground and joined Sera. "Watch out. More guards have arrived and it looks like they're preparing to launch the electric net. They know it worked on Arius last time."

Arius nodded his thanks, then released another spout of flame, taking out half a dozen targets this time. He cut off his fire and trembled, sagging a little.

"You need to stop," Sera exclaimed and fed him more energy. She stumbled as she realised how much of her own stores she'd fed to her Soulbound.

"So do you," he grunted. "I'm almost done. I must keep going."

She leant against his leg and breathed deeply. The report of gunfire sounded muffled. She shook her head, trying to clear it. After a moment, she asked, "What are we going to do about the net?"

"We need to get out of here as soon as we can so we don't need to deal with it," he replied.

Quill interrupted, "You focus on getting everyone out of here. Leave the net to me." The shadow disappeared, blending in with the night completely.

Negotiator Aaron stopped firing and stood, offering Sera his arm in support. "I'll help with getting everyone out of her—" His brows knitted together and he stared over Sera's shoulder. "What... Sera, look out!" He shoved her violently, forcing her to the ground. She landed hard, knocking her head, and the world tilted for a moment as she struggled to regain her senses.

"Aaron, what's wrong?" she pushed herself onto her knees and looked up at the Negotiator. Except, he wasn't there. She frowned as she swung her head, searching for him. Helena was suddenly right beside her, sending a hurried volley of shots off into the darkness, making her flinch, before turning around and looking at the ground behind Sera. The Head Tracker's shoulders slumped. Sera followed her gaze, a terrible sense of dread filling her, making her feel cold.

"Aaron?" she whispered.

The Negotiator was laying on his back, unmoving as a dark pool of liquid spread over his navy uniform.

"No." Her voice was hushed as she crawled toward him. "No," she repeated. Examining his shirt, she found the bullet hole that had ended his life. "He saved me," she whispered to no one in particular. "This isn't fair!" Her anguish ate a hole in her gut and she wrapped her arms around her middle, hoping it would keep herself from shattering.

Arius rumbled his sympathy. "He was a hero. And we will remember him. But I am afraid we can't shed tears for him yet. We need to leave now, Seraphina."

She nodded mutely, a numbing chill creeping through her limbs. She unwrapped her arms from her torso and gave her friend's hand one last squeeze before struggling to her feet, leaning on Arius' leg for support.

A loud screeching sound disrupted her spiralling and she gave a tormented cry. "What now?"

"Sounds like some sort of metal door," Allen muttered, pausing his shooting to scan the IRC grounds for the source.

In the middle yard, near the main building, a metal covering embedded in the earth was creaking back to reveal a hidden opening. Black hooks attached to leathery wings appeared, followed closely by a black dragon's head. Arius hissed through his teeth. "Desamor? But I thought we broke him?"

"This isn't possible," said Sera. "He was gone."

Arius' brother pulled himself out of the hole in jerky movements but his eyes had changed. They were icy blue.

"We all need to get out of here now," said Sera. "But I'm going to need you to look after my body, Arius. I'm going to try to connect with Desamor and figure out what has happened to him."

With difficulty, she pushed her consciousness away from Arius and, ignoring the swirling mass of auras littering the battleground, she sent her full power into Desamor's mind. She looked around in confusion. It was empty, just as she'd left it at the Mythic Relations Office. She pushed deeper, wading through the thick liquid that grabbed onto her legs and found the bright spot that indicated the second level. While Sera sunk deeper into Desamor's mind, the black dragon attacked her friends. There was no trace of thought to expose how he was making his decisions but his body continued to act; his jaws snapped and talons swiped, taking out her allies. The guttural bellow of one of the taurons as Desamor crushed his body pushed her to dive deeper into his mind. As she threw herself through his consciousness, she could tell he was still a husk of his former self with no sign of his well of magic.

*Perhaps their talent dies along with their soul?*

When she arrived in the third level and found the green sickly lines of control, another presence became apparent. The ball of black and grey energy held the reins, pulling on them brusquely, controlling the dragon's movements. Sera watched in confusion for a moment before rushing forward, unsure how to attack with her mind but allowing instinct to guide her as she barrelled into the other being. As she connected with it, she felt the familiar touch of Kaesus' mind.

*What are you doing?* she screamed, her words echoing back on herself as she spoke to a mind within a mind.

*I'm sorry that it's come to this, but you forced my hand.* Kaesus said apologetically. *I took some of your blood as a precaution and my Alchemists did some experimenting. They crafted an elixir where I can control the body of this dragon for a short time.*

*How?* she cried.

*It was quite easy, actually. Since I've been using your mother's blood to keep me from aging over the years, it was a simple matter of having my Alchemists adjust the formula to tap into your blood's magic. I was very interested to see what ability you possessed. I've been practising my control with this dragon over the past few hours and am very impressed.* He sighed, changing the direction of his thoughts. *I hoped I wouldn't need to use it but you've left me no choice. And in all our talks, dear daughter, you never mentioned your ability to control the dragons.*

*This is exactly why I didn't,* she screamed back at him. *What in the Four Gods' names do you think you're doing? This is wrong! You need to let him go.*

*I can't,* he said, an edge of mania creeping into his voice. *I can't let you get away. I need you by my side. You may not realise it yet but you were meant to bring great change. And now I know what that is. You were put here on this earth as my daughter to help me control dragonkind and keep the citizens of Mandar safe.*

*Don't you understand? The dragons belong to Mandar as well. We should be working with them, not trying to control them.*

*Dragons can't be worked with,* Kaesus said sadly, *I respect them and their power but I can't afford to let them take over. And that's exactly what they would do, if we give them the opportunity.*

*No, they wouldn't! Aren't you listening?*

*You're very sweet, Seraphina. You believe the best of people but I'm afraid I can't allow the dragons back into Mandar City. So, I have to do this.* He turned and hauled on Desamor's lines. The dragon leapt into the air and flew low, the wind from his wings buffeting the armies beneath him. He crashed through the interior chain-link fence that separated the high-security block from the rest of the IRC. Landing awkwardly, Kaesus marched Desamor toward Arius, who blew a spout of flame at his brother's body. Since Kaesus controlled his empty mind, Desamor no longer felt pain, meaning the fire did nothing to slow him. The black dragon's head darted out and seized the delicate membrane of Arius' wing, tearing it. Arius' bellow of pain spurred Sera into action. Incensed, she threw her mind forward and wrapped it around Kaesus', smothering him. His stolen talent wasn't a natural part of him, so she held the advantage. With her superior control, she snatched the reins from him and shoved the President's mind away. Pumping the black dragon's wings, they laboriously rose into the air, flying away from Arius and the sounds of battle.

Swiftly guiding Desamor's body away from the electrified boundary, she stared through his eyes at the fires burning below. Dozens of guards had fallen in the battle but there were still so many waiting to replace them. Despair threatened to overwhelm her as she flew upward, the wires of the dome inhibiting her view of the sky. Looking back, she could see Arius cradling her unconscious body in his claws, hindered by his wounded wings while still trying to protect her. He turned sharply and said something to her parents and they rushed onto his back. Constantine and his pack were still darting around the grounds, taking down guards where they could. The pack had dwindled down to only three wolves and Constantine appeared to be favouring a paw. A number of the Little Birds, including five humans, the three taurons and two more unicorns had fallen to the steady barrage of bullets. She could still feel Kaesus' presence pummelling her, trying in vain to wrestle back control, but she ignored him. Sera had flown Desamor's body as far up as the domed boundary allowed. She hovered there for a moment, being careful not to brush a wingtip against the wires, for fear of being struck by electricity or magical enchantments. Her heart twisted in grief as she surveyed the destruction spread out below.

Strength fading fast, Sera's control on the dragon slipped. Just before she released him, she used the last of her energy to shove Kaesus out of Desamor's mind.

# CHAPTER TEN

EXHAUSTED AND DISORIENTATED, SERA dragged herself from unconsciousness and tried to make sense of where she was. Wind rushed over her body, pimpling her skin. She shivered, wishing she had her jacket. Her eyelids felt so heavy, she couldn't summon the energy to open them. She shifted uncomfortably; she was laying on something uneven and hard. She frowned, struggling to shift the brain fog to figure out what was happening. With a groan, she forced her eyes open. Blinking, she turned her head and took a moment to absorb her situation. She was cocooned in Arius' talons as they flew low over the forest. Arius' wingbeats were laboured and she could hear him breathing heavily.

*Are you all right, Arius?* she whispered into his mind.

*Don't waste your strength on connecting with me, my Soulbound. We will land momentarily and I will explain everything,* he replied.

She withdrew thankfully, completely drained.

His wingbeats changed rhythm and they landed heavily in a small clearing. Arius crushed some shrubs on his arrival and sank to the ground with a grunt. He cradled Sera's body protectively as Allen hurried off his back, helping Elisabeth down.

Sera could hear Allen murmuring to her mother, "I can't believe you're here. I can't believe I didn't know. I'm so sorry."

"Hush, my love," Elisabeth replied. "You couldn't have known. I'm safe now."

"How could he do that to you?" Allen's voice choked around his rage.

"We need to focus on the future now and figure out our next step." Elisabeth placed a placating hand against Allen's arm, before turning away from him and approaching Sera.

Arius gently deposited his Soulbound on the ground, adjusting his position so she was sitting up against his foreleg.

"Are you all right, my darling?" Elisabeth asked, kneeling in front of her and staring into her eyes. Allen followed his wife and sat down on Sera's left side, squeezing her hand in silent support.

"Exhausted, but I don't think I'm hurt," she murmured sleepily and smiled at her parents.

"You did it, my darling girl," Elisabeth said happily. "We made it out of there."

"Not all of us." Sera's smile dimmed at the memory of Aaron's lifeless body. Tears streaked down her cheeks. She choked out her next words, feeling she owed it to him to make sure she wasn't the only one who remembered his kindness. "I didn't really spend much time with Aaron at the MRO but he was always nice to me. Then, in the IRC, he somehow got Arius unhooked from the drugs that were keeping him bound in his human form. And," she hiccoughed, "he made me smile in a place where I didn't think I could."

Arius pressed his scaled cheek against her right arm, offering his comfort. "He will be remembered. The stars see everything. Illundar will sing his praises to the ages."

Her mother gently wiped the tears from her cheeks. "I know how hard it is to lose a friend. You feel like there's a great emptiness inside you that wasn't there before. And you will feel terrible for a long time. But, I promise you, one day, you will be able to say his name with a smile and the pain... well, it never really goes away, but over time, it changes. It will become bearable. But, once all this is over, give yourself time to grieve." Elisabeth leant forward and embraced her tightly.

A round of sobs shook Sera's body, as her mother's touch released the tenuous hold she held over her emotions. After a long cry, Sera squeezed her mother and whispered hoarsely, "Thank you." As the pair separated, Arius shifted behind her and stifled a groan. Sera looked up with a frown. "You're hurt?" she asked.

"I'll be fine," he muttered. "Just give me some time to heal. And don't you dare think about giving me any more of your energy," he warned when he saw her scratching the golden scar on her palm. "You have already been weakened. And these injuries aren't life threatening for me."

"Fine," she grumbled before changing the subject. "What about everyone else? Balthazar, Tor, Helena, Quill, Constantine... the rest of the Little Birds? Did they make it out?" She bit her lip and waited with bated breath, praying for the safety of the rest of her friends. She didn't know whether she could handle any more loss tonight.

Arius replied swiftly, "They were fine when I saw them last. When you released Desamor's mind, his body fell onto the main block of the IRC, crushing the wall and freeing a large number of imprisoned mythics. They joined the battle and gave us the diversion we needed to escape. The Little Birds were disappearing into the forest when we flew away."

She breathed a sigh of relief and the tension that had been holding her rigid released, leaving her to sag against his leg. Turning her attention back to her parents, her heart squeezed from the outpouring of love. Never, in her wildest dreams, had she thought she would see them together again. "Mum, Dad." She smiled as they both looked at her. Her father had tears rolling down his cheeks.

"If this is a dream," he said, "I never want to wake up." He leant forward and kissed Elisabeth before squeezing Sera in a tight hug. She buried her head into his shoulder, beyond thankful to have her father safe in her arms.

*There were a few moments in there when I thought I'd never have this again.*

Allen pulled away and Elisabeth immediately took his place, cuddling her daughter again. "Sera, darling. You need to eat. You need to recover your strength."

Sera chuckled.

Elisabeth quirked an eyebrow. "What's so funny?"

"That's such a 'mum' thing to say... and, well, I've never really had that. I've seen the way Hazel's mum fusses over her but I've never really gotten to enjoy that myself."

"You'll never know how sorry I am that I wasn't there for you."

"It wasn't your fault, Mum." Sera raised her eyebrows. "Are you seriously still blaming yourself for Kaesus taking you?"

"I can't help it," her mother responded with a gentle shove against her shoulder. "Logically, I know there was nothing I could have done but as your mother I can't help thinking that I could have. Maybe I could have befriended Quill and escaped years ago?"

"Quill wasn't ready to switch sides until recently." Sera shook her head. "Stop blaming yourself."

"Why did the President take you, anyway?" Allen asked.

"Not long after Sera was born, he found something out about my heritage. He thought that I would be a 'valuable asset' to him," she added the air quotes with her fingers, "and he was right. He took my blood and had his Alchemists create an elixir that extended his life. He faked my death to avoid any inconvenient questions and kept me in that prison for years." She squeezed her eyes shut at the memory.

Allen's expression was murderous while he clenched his hands in agitation. "What did he find out about your heritage that would make him steal you away?"

Elisabeth's hand flew to her throat. "I'm sorry, my love. I cannot say." Turning back to Sera, she reprimanded, "I was serious though, you do need to eat." She looked around the clearing. "Do we even have any food?"

A loud crash interrupted their conversation.

As one, their heads swivelled towards the sound. Standing there, frozen in shock was Sera's grandmother, Del, her mouth making a small "o" as she stared at her daughter.

"Eli?" she whispered.

"Mama!" she cried and dashed forward.

"Eli!" cried Del again. Her wizened body shuddered with sobs as she folded her daughter into her arms. "I thought you were dead! How—" she didn't finish the sentence as she patted her daughter's gaunt body, fussing over her scrawniness.

Alistair appeared out of the trees from where Del had come from and picked up the backpack she'd dropped.

"Oh, yes. Alistair, come, come." She beckoned the gargoyle forward. "Of course, you know Sera already but this is my daughter Eli - Elisabeth - and my son-in-law, Allen. And I assume this can only be Arius." She gave a small bow and struggled to straighten. "It is an honour to meet you. And I am grateful for your protection of my granddaughter."

Arius remained reclined but nodded in return.

"Here," Del exclaimed, "I heard you saying you needed food. Alistair, give me a hand, will you?" She gestured to the mythic and he began opening the bag silently, pulling out skyberries, loaves of bread, a wheel of cheese and a cake tin.

Alistair nodded to Arius and said, "I will hunt for small game and return with your meal shortly." With that he melted into the trees, his mottled grey skin offering him excellent camouflage amongst the forest.

Arius called out his thanks but the gargoyle had already disappeared.

Giving the dragon a quizzical look, Allen asked, "Why don't you return to your human form and eat with us?"

"I am a dragon first, and a human second. When I transform into a human, it costs me energy to maintain it. Whilst my ability to hold that form for an extended period of time seems to have grown since Sera and I became Soulbound, it still exhausts me. I was already extremely fatigued after being bound as a human in the IRC, and, after burning through the wards on the fence, I was utterly spent. I will remain in my natural state for as long as I can to help me recover."

"Makes sense," Allen replied. "I'm glad you were strong enough to get us out of there. I owe you, not only my life, but the lives of my wife and daughter as well. Thank you, Arius."

The dragon bowed his head in acceptance of Allen's gratitude. As the humans all tucked in to their feast, a look of confusion passed over Arius' face as he scented the air.

Sera went on high alert and through a mouthful of food demanded, "What's wrong?"

"Nothing is... wrong, exactly. There is no danger at present. Although, I will say we shouldn't dally here too long. They'll be hunting us. It's just... your scent... it's..." He shook his head, clearly confused. "It's almost like..." he trailed off. Arius cast a puzzled look over the three generations of women and cocked his head.

Del went to say something but reached her hand to her throat as she gagged. She turned pleading eyes to Sera. "I can't tell you anything," she said, frustration etched in the lines of her face. "I desperately want to but I'm not allowed. You'll have to figure it out for yourself."

Sera looked between her grandmother and mother. They shared a pained look but remained mute.

Arius spoke slowly as he mulled over his words. "Sera has a particular scent that drew me to her from the first moment we met. It reminds me of my kind."

"What do you mean, 'your kind?'" Allen asked.

"What I mean, is that she smells like a dragon. Once we became Soulbound I just put it down to that. But now you're all here I can smell the same scent from your mother and grandmother." He snaked his head toward the circle of humans and took a deep breath. "But not from Allen."

She contemplated Arius and thought back on the last conversation she's had with Del, when her grandmother had hinted at mythic bloodlines.

"What?" Sera scoffed. "The only explanation that fits is that we have dragon blood. But that's impossible."

Del whined, unable to say anything.

"You can't be serious?" Sera exclaimed. But even as she said the words, it all slotted into place. She didn't understand how, but in her heart, she knew the truth. She was dragonkind.

# CHAPTER ELEVEN

ALISTAIR STEPPED OUT OF the trees then and placed three dead pheasants and a small deer in front of Arius. With a grateful nod of thanks, the dragon immediately began wolfing down the carcasses.

Ignoring the sound of crunching from her Soulbound, and not ready to deal with the fact she was part-dragon, Sera said to the gargoyle, "That was quick."

Alistair flashed her a grin before picking up the second backpack and walking toward her, the tips of his wings dragging along the earth. Sera stood when she realised it was her own pack from where she had stashed it in the tree trunk before entering the IRC. She shot him a questioning look. He simply placed it in front of her and gestured to the side pocket. Opening it, she pulled out her Seeing Stone. Elisabeth and Del came closer and looked over her shoulder.

Sera shot an accusatory glare at the gargoyle. *Here I am, trying desperately to hold onto a semblance of sanity by not addressing my ancestry, and here he is, forcing me to face it, head on.* Cupping the stone in the palm of her hand, Sera watched it and held the question of her lineage in her mind. Sapphire blue feathers filled the surface before zooming out to show a beautiful dragon. She was all soft lines and elegance, with no scales to be seen. Sera froze as she recognised the feathers. Bending down, she dug through her pack again and found the blue feather the President had left her.

Del cried out a garbled word but grabbed her throat as her oath prevented her from speaking.

Sera looked between the Seeing Stone, the feather and her Nanna. "Was this... your mother's?"

Tears filled the old woman's eyes as she nodded.

"Wow," Sera breathed as she admired her great-grandmother in wonder. A sudden thought flitted into her mind to prove the family secret. First, she reached her mind out and brushed against her mother's, again noting the soft golden glow flecked with spots of iridescent blue.

Elisabeth started and looked around fearfully.

*It's just me.*

*Sera?* Elisabeth gave her an incredulous look. *Was that you who I sensed in the IRC?*

*Yes.* Testing her abilities, she gently drew her grandmother's aura into her contact, realising as she did that her Nanna's aura was similar in colour to both her mother's and her own. *Hi Nanna, it's Sera. Can you both hear me?*

Both her mother and grandmother nodded, eyes wide in amazement.

*This is my talent. I can speak telepathically with dragons and I can also delve deeper and take control. I try not to do that too often though.* Sera winced at the sickening memory of breaking Desamor's mind. *That's how Kaesus managed to take over Desamor's body. He stole my blood while I was unconscious and used it like he used yours, Mum.*

*Amazing!* Del replied.

*It really is.* Elisabeth joined in.

Sera looked at her mother. *Did you hear Nanna's response just then?*

They looked at each other and nodded.

*Have you ever connected to each other in the past?* Sera probed.

*No,* replied Elisabeth, whilst Del shook her head.

*Huh. Let me try something else.* Thankful for the energy boost the skyberries had given her, she touched Arius' mind too. *Arius, can you please see whether you can speak to Mum or Nanna through our connection?*

He paused his feasting and cocked his head curiously. *Certainly. Greetings to you both. Please excuse my horrendous table manners, I'm rather hungry after our little visit to the prison.*

Del sniggered and Elisabeth gave him a sympathetic look before saying, *I know what you mean. They like to keep you half-starved in that place.*

Clapping her hands in excitement, Sera beamed at the unexpected extension to her talent. *So, it seems I can create a mind link between other dragons as well, so long as I remain a part of the connection.*

Sending a puff of smoke her way, Arius said, *That would come in handy in a battle.*

The sound of wingbeats interrupted their internal conversation and Sera released the connection before spinning around with Firinne at the ready. When she recognised the two hippogryphs coming into land, she immediately relaxed and sheathed her blade.

"Tor!" Sera cried and rushed forward to embrace her friend. "You're safe."

"Yes," he panted but tucked his head over her shoulder, returning her hug. Stepping back, he gave his body a shake and said, "You will all have to leave soon. The President was delayed by the outpouring of escaped mythics but he was preparing to leave when we flew away."

"We just stopped to eat and rest for a moment. But we'll be on our way soon."

The hippogryph nodded. "Good."

Before he said anything more, Sera interrupted him, "Tor... I'm sorry about your father. Tormund was a wonderful teacher and a good friend of mine."

"And mine," added Alistair.

"Before he died, he asked me to tell you something. He wanted you to know that he always loved you." She stroked his feathers, admiring the way they shone silver in the moonlight. Her heart broke for him as he keened his loss to the sky.

"I missed him when Mother banished him. She always said he and I were too alike for my own good." He chuckled through his tears. "She was right, I guess."

A caw split the night and Del held her arm up as Fray appeared and landed on her offered hand. The raven bobbed his head. "Charming to see you again, Seraphina. Charming!" he croaked. "I hate to break up the party but you'll need to get a move on post-haste. A small team of guards including the President left the IRC ten minutes ago. They are astride their unicorn mounts. The unicorns have combined their power and are tracing Arius' magic trail. It is a slower way to track, but very effective. They will find you in short order. There is still much fighting on the grounds of the Iniques Rehabilitation Centre. Much fighting! When the black dragon's body crashed onto the building, it collapsed two walls, releasing perhaps a hundred mythics. Some are frail and unable to fight but those that can are certainly making up for them. Many are dead but many have escaped into the forest. The dragon's body was broken in his fall and his heart failed so the President won't be able to control him again."

Sera sent a silent prayer of thanks to the Gods for granting them one win.

"We never planned on causing a mass break out, but it's certainly worked in our favour," mused Arius, picking his teeth clean with a claw.

Sera clasped her head tightly in her hands and fought against the overwhelming pressure that threatened to drown her. There had been so many emotions and so much new information revealed in a short space of time, it made her sway from the enormity of it all. Taking a few deep, steadying breaths, she turned to Arius.

"I need to focus on one thing at a time or I'm not going to make it through. Our new priority is to get everyone to safety. So, what's the plan now?

Alistair stepped forward and said, "I can craft a tunnel to take the humans to wherever they need to go." He looked at Arius sizing him up. "I could make a tunnel for you but it will take a lot longer given your size. I would recommend that you travel by wing, if possible."

Arius bowed his head in agreement. Sera ran a critical eye over his body.

"Are you well enough to fly?" she asked.

"I will admit I'm not running at my full capacity but I have enough energy to get you and I away from here. I don't think I could manage another flight with multiple passengers though."

"Okay." Sera laced her hands together as she considered their current predicament. She spoke her thoughts aloud. "So, the President is chasing after us. He won't be easily dissuaded so we need to find a way to convince him to drop the hunt. But more than that," she tapped her chin with her finger, "what I saw in there…" She shuddered. "They're harvesting mythics for their own sick gains." Shaking her head, she continued, "It's not right. We can't just run away and leave those that didn't escape to suffer for the rest of their lives. We have to fight this." Swivelling on her foot, she planted her hands on her hips and levelled Arius with an intense stare. "Is there any chance that we could convince the dragons of Sky Valley to reveal themselves to the citizens of Mandar City?" She held up her finger. "But not to attack. I would not want innocent lives lost because of the dragons. We need to foster trust and honesty between humans and the mythics of Mandar. We need to show the people that the President has been lying all along. That dragons still exist and have been shunned by society and hidden away for their own safety. We don't need to be enemies. We need to prove that to them. But how?" She tapped her chin as she mulled over the future. "Humans do love their official paperwork. If we could arrange for the Peace Covenant to be updated and re-signed, that should hold all parties to their promise."

Arius nodded thoughtfully. "If we can get my father on our side, then yes, I believe that we can convince the Elders to witness the signing but not attack. Especially since you're the one spoken of in the prophecy."

"I'm not the prophesied one. I'm not anyone special, I'm just trying to do the right thing."

Arius chuckled lightly. "Not anyone special, she says. Hah! How many decades has it been since the mythics have been abused by those in power and no one has done anything to stop it. You are special, Seraphina. And I love you for it. Caelhi blessed me the day she chose you as my Soulbound."

Sera blushed and folded her arms. "If it means the dragons will follow me, then fine. I'll be your blooming prophesied one, if that's what it takes. Arius and I will travel to Sky Valley to ask the dragons to sign the new treaty." She glanced at her parents and ducked her head bashfully when she saw the pride shining from their eyes.

Del said, "We will locate the Little Birds and tell them the plan. We will see what we can do to distract the President's forces so that you have time to return with the dragons."

Sera shot her a look. "You know about the Little Birds—" but cut herself off with a shake of her head. There had been too many revelations in the past few days for her to be surprised anymore. "All right, sounds like a plan. Tell their leader, Urma, that Seraphina sent you."

Del nodded her understanding before sorting the backpacks. She muttered, "If I'd known you'd be traveling so far, I would have packed more food for the journey."

Alistair announced, "I will go with you, Del. It's time I returned to the Little Birds." He grasped Sera's shoulder, his hand heavy. "After I helped to return your memories, I travelled underground to the country of my brethren."

"I didn't know there was a country for your kind! I haven't seen many other gargoyles in my travels around Mandar," said Sera in wonder.

"We're around. If you know where to look. We conferred for two days and two nights until the leaders agreed to gather our forces and offer our support to the Little Birds' cause. Should it come to war, the gargoyles will be ready. But I will pray to the Four Gods that your plan for a peaceful end to this conflict works." He grinned at Sera before raising his gravelly voice and flared his wings. "May this be the anti-war to end all anti-wars." He gave her shoulder a comforting squeeze. "Good luck. The hopes of all mythics fly with you." He turned around and began weaving his hands slowly through the air, before placing them on the ground. His magic shimmered, creating a pool of liquid earth as tiny specks of blue lit up all over his body. A fissure ran through the dirt and widened, creating a tunnel for Sera's family.

Del, Elisabeth and Allen each came forward and gave her a hug and multiple kisses on the cheek.

Allen rubbed her back and murmured, "I'm so proud of you." He shrugged out of his jacket and wrapped it around her shoulders. "You need this more than I do."

Elisabeth held her hand and whispered, "Please be safe, darling. We'll be waiting for you when you return."

"You be safe, too," she choked out as she held them in her arms.

"Time to go," cawed Fray, hopping anxiously on Del's shoulder.

Reluctantly releasing them, Sera wiped the tears from her cheeks and asked, "What will you do, Tor?"

"I'm going to return to my flock to speak with my mother about the events that have transpired this night."

Sera's brows pulled together and she opened her mouth to ask whether that was a good idea but Tor cut her off.

"I know she banished me and threatened to execute me should I ever return, but this is bigger than family. This is about the lives of all mythics. I pray to Caelhi that my mother will hear me out. If it does come to war, you'll need all the support you can get. Hopefully it doesn't and the flock can merely witness a renewed signing of the Peace Covenant. Bels, I need you to travel with Seraphina and Arius."

"What? Why?" demanded the bay hippogryph. "I want to stay with you."

"I know you do. There will be time for us later. Arius and Sera are weak and they have a long way to travel. If you go with them, or, at least part of the way, then you can help with fetching water and food for them both."

Bels gave an irritated shake of her head. "You want me to serve the human?"

Tor glowered at her. "If you don't want to be a part of helping forge new alliances between mythics and humans, then you can leave now and don't bother showing your face again."

Bels dropped her head and looked at the ground. "I'll help," she muttered sullenly.

Meanwhile, Sera's grandmother said to Arius, "Fly fierce. I hope we meet again one day when all this is over."

The dragon blew a puff of smoke and pressed his snout to Del's chest. "As do I, Del. It is an honour to have met you. Strike strong, my friend."

With one last tearful goodbye, the three humans and the gargoyle traipsed down the tunnel, disappearing quickly from view.

# CHAPTER TWELVE

PLANS FORMED, AND FAREWELLS delivered, Arius, with Sera aboard, leapt into the air, Bels following close behind. They flew swiftly and remained close to the tree-tops, praying to the Four Gods that the meagre cover of night would keep them safe from prying eyes. Sera watched over her shoulder and waved as Tor broke off and headed for Lake Eyre. She hoped his mother would be forgiving and he'd be safe.

Her eyes flicked to Bels', who glared at her. Sera dropped her gaze, confused by the animosity the hippogryph had shown her since discovering she and Arius were Soulbound all those weeks ago. As they left the gentle slopes surrounding the IRC behind, Arius adjusted his flight path to make use of the thermals to help him gain altitude over the Mandar Ranges. Sera could feel the fatigue and pain dragging at her Soulbound so she sent him energy through their bond. He shook his head so she connected with him.

*What's wrong, Arius?*

*I don't want you expending all your energy to keep me airborne.*

*I have a little to spare,* she grumbled. *And anyway, you've fed me energy in the past when you shouldn't have,* she countered.

*Well, yes, I have, but it's different.*

*How is it different, Arius? Yes, we are Soulbound but, more than that, we're also partners. That means we give and take equally. You've got to get it out of your head that you have to be the one rescuing me all the time.*

*Yes, but I'm a dragon. I can protect you. Will you let me?*

*Of course I'll let you, so long as you return the favour.*

He muttered something out loud but the wind stole it away. *Fine,* he replied in her mind. *I understand what you're saying and I respect your wishes to not be treated like a damsel in distress.*

She smirked. *Thank you.* She pushed a little more of her energy his way and he grunted his thanks. *That a little better?*

*Enough to keep me going,* he admitted, then added. *Please, distract me. I might be able to fly further if I'm not focussed on how tired I feel.*

*I can do that.* Remembering something she'd promised to explain, she said, *Remember, in the IRC, when I said fuck a duck? It's an expression humans use to indicate anger or surprise. It's considered a rude term in most circles but I felt the situation called for it.*

He chuckled weakly. *Thank you for the clarification. I must admit, I was very concerned about what you were suggesting was going to happen to a duck. That makes sense now.*

Sera laughed as the wind whipped over them, stirring her hair. She dreaded the next time she had to brush it. It would be a tangled mess. Running her hands over her locks in an attempt to flatten them, she launched into the story of everything that had happened after Arius had been captured. Her constant chattering seemed to ease the tension in her dragon's body as they travelled over the ranges.

They flew on through the night, Arius' efforts to maintain the pace becoming more laboured as the hours wore on. Sera had zipped her father's jacket up at the beginning of their flight, but she was still freezing. Her fingers had grown numb and she pressed them to her dragon's scales in the hopes his internal warmth would thaw them. Fatigue pulled at her limbs but she was afraid to sleep while she knew Arius' exhaustion matched her own. They were over the Red Waste when Sera noticed Arius was flying closer than he should to the dunes.

"Arius!" she called out over the wind. "How about we take a break?"

"We can't stop here," he called back. "It's the Red Waste, there's nothing around for miles."

"You can't keep going like this," she said. "And I no longer have enough spare energy to lend you."

A strong gust of wind swept up over a sand dune causing Arius to wobble. He flapped a few times to correct when another gust hit him, forcing him to veer off course to avoid smacking into the ground.

"All right, you win!" he shouted in frustration. He slowed and adjusted his trajectory, bringing his hind legs down to land, followed by the front. Sera's breath left her in a whoosh when they jolted to the ground, her fatigue getting the better of her, as she smacked into the spine in front. He raised a trembling foreleg close to his neck to give her an easier dismount and she clambered swiftly off his back. The night was surprisingly cold in the desert and Sera rubbed her arms and stomped her feet, trying to get feeling and warmth back into them. Bels landed nearby and without meeting their eyes said, "I suppose I'll go find some food and water for you then, shall I?"

Sera said, "I don't know how much luck you'll have around here. But don't worry about the water, we've got some full bottles in the backpack. But if you can find any extra food, we would be very grateful."

The hippogriff gave a jerky nod and cantered away, the sand making her work hard to take off, before leaping back into the air.

"Thank you!" Sera called out after her. Bels ignored her and disappeared into the night.

Sera glanced around at what had looked to be barren land from the air but now noticed the dead tree, boulder and occasional skeleton peeking through the red sand. Arius took a deep breath before blasting a stream of fire onto the blackened trunk that lay nearby. It immediately caught alight and Sera sidled closer to the warmth.

Arius groaned and collapsed onto his side. "If you're still cold," he murmured, "just cuddle up to me." He yawned, his fangs glinting in the firelight. "I'm going to get some sleep now." His eyes drifted shut.

Sera sat, chewing her lip, watching his chest as the breathing slowed and deepened. Sleep would help him recover but she could help his natural healing along a little. She dug through her pack and found the container of Heal and began applying it to his wings. They had received a battering, with many lesions to the membrane. Taking her time, she applied the cream to the worst of his injuries, knowing that he would heal himself and unsure if they would need the balm for future battles before she would have the chance to stock up again.

*If I can even stock up again. What happens now? When all this is over, will I ever be allowed back at the MRO? Do I even want to go back?*

Scrounging through the backpack again, she found the last of the bread and cheese that Del had packed. She sat with her back to Arius' chest, warming herself from his inner heat and munched on her food. While she waited for the hippogryph to return, she took a swig of her water canteen and contemplated their future.

*The concept of the MRO to foster healthy relationships between humans and mythics is a good one. But it's been corrupted over time. It's now a way of control. They need a new system in place with equal opportunities for both mythics and humans.*

As she leaned her head back against Arius' body and pondered these tricky questions for the future, the grief she'd kept at bay unexpectedly hit her in the gut. The death of Aaron, especially so close on the heels of losing Tormund, was debilitating. Tears fell as she mourned her friends. The hole inside of her heart was back, demanding to be felt. She cried for a long time. The muffled sound of hoofbeats had her hurriedly wiping her face and standing up.

Bels had landed nearby with a mouthful of fur which she tossed to the ground in front of Sera.

"I found some rabbits, if you're hungry?"

"Where did you find them? I thought no animals lived in the Red Waste," Sera asked, surprise colouring her tone.

"The clever blighters know that not many creatures come to the desert so they built a warren near the boundary. They enjoy relative safety from predators but can still forage in the forest."

"You flew all the way back to the edge of the Waste?" Sera exclaimed. "Thank you."

"Well, Tor told me it was my duty to help you and this should help. Don't read too much into it." She harrumphed and turned away from Sera.

Sera ignored her unfriendly demeanour and closed the gap between them when she noticed a bloody cut on her flank. Her hands flew to her mouth. "You're hurt, Bels! Why didn't you say something?"

The hippogriff shrugged a shoulder. "It's not too bad."

"Here, let me help."

Bels stood stiffly while Sera applied the Heal cream. But once Sera had stopped her ministrations, Bels sighed and her head drooped, the tension suddenly leaving her body.

"Thank you for that," said the hippogryph.

Sera wiped the greasy residue off her hands and onto her grey pants before approaching the mare's head. "Bels," she said gently, "I want to understand what I've done wrong. When we last met, you followed Tor into his banishment and said that you would support both he and I. But when you found out that Arius and I were Soulbound, you become, at best, cold toward me, and, at worst, openly hostile. I don't understand why things changed."

Bels shook her head in agitation and stamped her hoof. "It's complicated," she hedged.

"If the reason is too personal, I'll understand if you don't want to talk about it. I just want you to know that I'm here for you too. Tor is my friend and you are his. You're willing to help us, even though it seems like that goes against your personal beliefs. I just want you to know that I'm grateful. And I'm here if you want to talk."

Bels sighed heavily and followed Sera to where she sat down near the fire, skinning the rabbits. The hippogryph folded her legs and lay down quietly behind her, just out of reach of the fire's circle of light.

She spoke softly and Sera kept her eyes focussed on the task at hand. She didn't dare interrupt while the mythic spoke.

"Since the Mythic War, my flock— or rather, my old flock—has been vaguely aware that perhaps not all dragons were dead. However, we did not know that there was a whole valley of them hidden away. Dragons were always spoken of in the highest respect. We revered them, almost as if they were Gods. And whilst the Peace Covenant had been signed, humans and hippogryphs have never been close friends. And, as a general rule, we consider your kind to be dirty, loud and obnoxious." She tipped her head to Sera. "I apologise for that. I know we shouldn't tar you all with the same feather. Let me try and explain it in your terms. Imagine if your Goddess Ghaia married your President, whom I assume you consider a lowly human since you escaped from his prison. Would that not shock you? Would you not be outraged? How could a God choose to join with one such as him?"

Sera tilted her head and considered Belisa's comparison. "It's a difficult concept to wrap my head around," she answered after a long moment. "So, yes, I suppose I can understand your shock."

Without getting up, Belisa shuffled awkwardly forward so she was closer to Sera. "And also," she grinned sheepishly, "I will admit that I was already trying to stifle my jealousy of your friendship with Torvold and when I found out you were Soulbound to another mythic... The shock of finding out released my tenuous control and I allowed my jealousy to bubble over into anger. As much as it pains me to admit it, you're a good human, Seraphina, and I am willing to follow you." She nudged Sera's shoulder playfully with her beak. "Please accept my apologies for my immature behaviour."

Sera laughed, relieved to be on friendly terms with the mythic finally. "That makes me happy." She reached up and scratched behind the hippogryph's feathery ear in her hard to reach spot. Bels sighed happily and leaned into the contact.

After finishing the skinning, she skewered one of the carcasses on a stick and began cooking hers. "Here, Bels, have this one. You need your energy too. I'll leave the other two for Arius when he wakes." She passed one of the rabbits toward her new friend. The hippogryph began tearing into the gamey meat.

After they'd finished their meal, Bels said, "Get some rest. I'll take the first shift and I'll wake you in a few hours."

# CHAPTER THIRTEEN

SERA STARTLED AWAKE AT the feel of something hard pushing against her shoulder. Her hand automatically grasped Firinne and she sat up but relaxed when she saw Belisa's familiar face.

"I tried calling your name but you slept so soundly, I had to touch you. Sorry for giving you a fright." She glanced at the sky. "I gave you as much sleep as I could, Seraphina," whispered the hippogriff. "While I may not need as much sleep as a human, it's been a long day, so I will ask that you take your watch now."

"Of course," Sera said. "Get some rest, Bels."

"There was no sign of movement during the past four hours," she reported. "Dawn should be here soon. I have heard of scorpius roaming the deserts of a daytime, so keep an eye out for them once the sun rises."

"Thank you, Bels, sleep well."

The hippogryph gave a tired smile. "As you wish." She lay down near the campfire and, closing her eyes, was asleep within seconds.

Sera stood with a yawn and stretched, her heartbeat finally returning to a normal rhythm after being frightened awake. She walked around the massive form of Arius, scanning his injuries in the weak light. She was pleased to see that most were showing signs of healing well. The night sky was a deep purple with stars peppering it with their feeble light. The moon hung low, tracking its familiar path toward the horizon, leaving behind a silvery wash over everything it touched. The emptiness of the Red Waste stretched out for miles around them. Due to the position of the constellations, she knew that if she travelled due East, she would eventually make it to Mandar City. She couldn't help but be thankful for her dragon, she would hate to traverse this endless expanse on foot alone with limited supplies. She grabbed her bottle of water out of the backpack and drank deeply. Her lips felt so dry, the climate harsh, even at night. Pulling her jacket closer around her, she picked up a brisk walk around the camp to keep herself warm. She mulled over everything that had happened and contemplated her dragon ancestors. It was such an unbelievable discovery, yet she could feel the truth of it in her very being. Two months ago, she had been Sera. Just Sera. Trying to live her life as a Tracker and now here she was, supposedly meant to be some prophesied saviour. No one ever expected to wake up one day and find out they were supposed to save the world and give mythics a voice since she was part-dragon and part-human. She shook her head.

*Absolutely insane.*

She slowed her march as she thought and stared, unseeing, into the distance. She gave herself a mental shake and refocussed her attention on her sentry duty again. The scent of decay reached her before she noticed anything else. Spinning around, she pulled Firinne swiftly from its sheath and glared into the darkness, raising the blade in preparation to throw it at an attacker. A figure exited from a shining portal. She sucked in a breath to yell for help but her tongue stuck to the roof of her mouth. She tried to throw Firinne at the figure but the staghorn handle remained fused to her hand. She screamed internally at the harpy's ability to immobilise her.

"That was impressive," the harpy said with a smirk. "Not many could take down the IRC." She held up her hands. "Calm your feathers, I just want to talk."

*Hard to talk when my mouth is glued shut.* Sera glowered at the harpy.

"If you promise not to yell, I promise to release you. And I swear I won't harm you." She rolled her eyes. "Provided, of course, that you don't try and stab me, or something stupid. Deal?"

Sera stared at her in exasperation. Whether she wanted to or not, she couldn't agree to the deal while she was frozen. The harpy appeared to realise that at the same time and chuckled. Sera sucked in a deep breath as the invisible bands wrapping around her neck released.

"Sorry about that." The harpy sat down with a thump and held her hands up in the universal sign of surrender. "Truce?"

Sera hesitated but eventually gave a curt nod. She spoke quietly to avoid waking the others, "I accept your deal. For now." The rest of her body thawed and she shook out her arms, uncomfortable with the feeling of being frozen. She chose to stay standing, Firinne in hand, not willing to fully trust the harpy.

"By the way, I haven't had a chance to properly introduce myself," said the harpy with a smile. The razor-sharp teeth that were revealed did nothing to put Sera at ease. "I'm Zaraxthün. But you can call me Zara." She rubbed the back of her neck, almost looking ashamed. "Look, I'm going to cut straight to the chase. I'm... sorry," she rasped the word through gritted teeth, "for my previous actions involving you. I always vowed I'd never get involved in the petty battles of the human world. That all changed when Kaesus captured my family. I had no choice. I had to save them. But then," she punctuated her sentence with a heavy sigh, "I couldn't. Kaesus kept my mate and my clutch from me. He found ways to hurt me with magic and kept me under his thumb for years. I've followed his orders in a bid to keep my family safe. Turns out, he crushed my eggs months ago to use in one of his precious potions." She spat out the word, hatred twisting the features of her beautiful face. She tugged on her dark hair, half covering her face while she composed herself. "But, when you dropped that dragon and destroyed those walls in the IRC, you gave me the opportunity to save my mate. Our children may be gone but at least we have each other." With that, another portal opened and the blue-haired harpy that Sera had noticed when they first entered the IRC stepped through.

Zara waved a hand toward him and said, "This is Xoran. He won't be talking much since Kaesus cut out his tongue." Her feathers bristled at the pain caused to her partner. Sera blanched at her biological father's cruelty. "But he wants me to pass on his gratitude. He wants to fight with you, but I don't. I'm sorry, Seraphina. Of course, I'm furious with Kaesus, but I'm so afraid of losing my last loved one. That man has taken everything else away from me. So, I choose to walk away from the human world and keep us safe. I hope you understand."

"I don't have children of my own, so I can only imagine your pain. But yes, I can understand wanting to keep your loved ones safe at all costs."

"Though I won't fight, I will offer you some advice. Over the years, Kaesus has siphoned off the magic of so many mythics that he's become near indestructible. Go for his heart with that magic knife of yours, then burn his body so there's no coming back. Your blade should undo the enchantments in his blood."

Sera grimaced at the grisly image but nodded. "Got it. Once he's out of the picture, I'll help facilitate an updated Peace Covenant that allows mythics the same rights as humans."

"Yeah, yeah, that's great to have all those high and mighty plans, but just... kill him for me, would you?" The harpies both nodded to Sera and, hand-in-hand, opened a portal, stepped through and disappeared from Mandar forever.

# CHAPTER FOURTEEN

WATCHING THE EMBERS SLOWLY snuff out in the dawn light, Sera's resolve hardened. There was no time left to doubt herself or her abilities anymore. She was dragonkind. She promised herself she would find a way to convince the Elders of Sky Valley to leave their seclusion and join their cause. They needed to prove to the people of Mandar City that dragons were real, and they meant humans no harm. If she failed, the best outcome she could hope for was that the rights of the mythics would be doomed to stay in the dark ages. And the worst outcome would involve the death of so many of her friends and loved ones. *I will not fail.*

Belisa yawned and stretched before standing with a grunt. She gave herself a shake, sand floating from her brown coat. "All quiet over the past few hours?" she queried, stifling another yawn.

"Not exactly," hedged Sera. "Hang on, I want to tell Arius too." She stood up, her back cracking, and approached Arius' head, but the sound of her speaking his name had already done the job.

He opened his eyes, followed by a few slow blinks. He gave a great yawn, his ivory white fangs gleaming in the morning light. Licking his lips, he asked, "What is it you wanted to tell me?"

Sera placed her hands on her hips combatively and began. "Now, don't freak out but the harpy visited in the early hours of this morning."

Her dragon leapt to his feet and there was an explosion of sound as both Arius and Bels began shouting at her. She blinked at the wall of sound. Their voices overtook one another but Sera got the gist that they were both pissed off she hadn't woken them.

Sera held her hands up and said, "Okay, okay, I get it. I would be peeved too. But before we get too carried away, please listen to what she had to say."

Arius snarled, "We should never listen to a harpy."

"Her name is Zara," Sera corrected.

"I don't care what her name is!" Arius rumbled. "She could have hurt you!"

"But she didn't!" Sera interrupted. "I would have woken you," Sera explained, "but she froze me before I realised what was happening. She promised to release me if I swore to do her no harm. So, I agreed." She shrugged.

Arius bared his fangs angrily but kept his mouth shut.

"Zara told me that when I took over Desamor's mind and he fell into the IRC, she was able to save her mate, Xoran, whom Kaesus has kept hostage for years. Zara recently found out that Kaesus had killed her children, so, once she had her mate safe, she escaped to get out from under his control."

At the mention of the harpy's lost children, Bels' beak dropped open, horror filling her eyes.

Sera continued, "She simply wanted to tell me that her and her partner bear us no ill will. We are safe from them. She also said she hopes we kill the President for what he did to her and her family. She told me the best way to kill Kaesus is to stab him in the heart with Firinne and then burn his body. Firinne's magical properties should dissolve the magic he's stolen from the mythics over the years. She and Xoran will not be participating in the battle and have already left the country.

Arius sat down heavily on his haunches and simply said, "Huh."

Bels glanced at him, then at Sera before saying, "While I don't agree with you putting yourself at risk, that was very helpful information she shared with you. And I'll admit I'm glad she's not in the fight anymore. Harpies are hard to kill."

Arius gave himself a shake. "Well, then," he said, "It's time we continued on our journey. Bels, I think it would be best if you left us here. Sky Valley is kept a secret among our kind and I do not wish to anger the Elders by bringing both a human and a hippogryph to their home."

Bels bowed. "I understand. I shall return to Tor and see if he requires my assistance in settling the flock. I will share with the Queen the fact that your actions convinced the harpy to abandon the President. It may be enough to tip the scales in our favour. Fly well, Seraphina and Arius. I pray to Caelhi for your safe journey and victorious return."

"Thank you, Bels," Sera said and wrapped her arms around her feathery neck in a hug. Bels stiffened for a moment before relaxing and drawing her wing around Sera, returning the embrace. "You stay safe too," whispered Sera and stroked her head.

Releasing Sera, Bels turned away and, with one last smile tossed over her shoulder, took off.

Arius gulped down the rabbits Sera had kept aside for him while she swung her backpack over her shoulders. Once he'd finished eating, she clambered up Arius' side and sat behind one of his spines. They launched into the sky and, once Arius had gained enough altitude and settled into his flight, Sera connected with his mind.

*How are you feeling this morning anyway? You were too busy yelling at me earlier for me to ask.*

He chuckled. *I feel much better, thank you, my beloved. The injuries are fast on their way to recovery and I am well rested. Although, I do feel guilty for not taking a turn guarding the campsite.*

*Don't be silly,* she chided. *You're my ride. I need you at full strength.*

He snorted. *I hope I'm more than just a ride.*

She sniggered at the innuendo, then leant forward and embraced his neck, her arms not even half way round. *You know you are.* Changing the subject, she asked, *Where is Sky Valley anyway?*

*If I told you I'd have to kill you,* he responded solemnly, then laughed. *I'm joking, of course. Decades ago, at the end of the war, the dragons combined their magic to create a portal into the hidden valley. If anyone were to wander near it, they'd simply think it was an electrical storm and avoid the area. Even if they were stupid enough to brave the storm, it is unlikely they would gain access. You have to travel at great speeds to enter the portal.*

As they flew on in silence, Sera ran through scenarios in her head of what she could say to convince the dragons, both of her lineage and her need for their help. Every speech she came up with seemed weaker than the last. She buried her face in her hands and blew out a frustrated sigh.

*I'm scared, Arius. What if I can't convince them?*

*Do not fear, my love. We will find a way. Trust in yourself. Trust in us. For now, though, prepare yourself. We're headed for a bumpy flight.*

Pumping his wings fiercely, Arius flew faster and faster, the air streaming over their bodies. Dark clouds closed in around them and lightning crackled in her periphery. Sera's eyes watered as the wind buffeted her and she clung grimly onto the spine in front of her.

They flew toward a churning funnel of cloud and Sera screamed, "What are you doing? We'll be killed!"

He ignored her and increased his speed. As they flew closer to the terrifying vortex, rain stung her exposed skin. Sera squeezed her eyes closed and gritted her teeth, waiting to be torn from Arius' body. When the wind suddenly stopped snatching at her, she opened her eyes and gasped. They were entering the gaping eye of the vortex. Purple clouds swirled around them with rainbow sparks spinning along the edges. Her mouth fell open as she marvelled at the magical phenomenon. It was surreal. In a dreamlike state, she reached a hand out toward the wall of the funnel and one of the sparks danced up her arm playfully. The hairs on the back of her arms stood up as it twirled around her, flashing through every colour Sera had ever seen along with some new ones. Just as she was about to connect to Arius and ask how long they would stay in the enchanted tunnel, they burst out the end of it.

# CHAPTER FIFTEEN

SERA SUCKED IN A sharp intake of breath at the scene laid out before her. The sun hung low in the sky, illuminating the dozens of dragons moving through the valley the portal had deposited them in. Wingless dragons snaked their way through the sky, bouncing around the puffy clouds. The sunlight refracted rainbows from the fish-like scales that covered their serpentine bodies, their beauty making Sera's heart soar. A small hillock nearby unexpectedly moved. Sera squeaked in astonishment and peered closer. What had, on first glance, appeared to be an earthy mound was in fact an enormous drake. The huge mythic was at least twice the size of Arius and moved slowly across the landscape, each step leaving heavy claw prints in the ground. Each scale was a shade of slate grey or a soft mossy green. Upon closer inspection, it seemed that there was indeed some living moss growing on its body. Beady yellow eyes glanced in her direction and the creature snorted in shock. It considered Arius for a moment then turned away and lumbered onward.

Eyes bugging, Sera slowly dismounted onto the rocky outcrop they'd landed on and stared in awe at the magnificence around her. A small tremor of branches in a copse of trees to their right caught her eye. She could just make out a dark green wyvern that blended in with the forest. She caught a glimpse of a sunset orange eye as it snaked its head forward to observe her. Its antlers imitated tree branches but the mythic moved its head in such a way as to avoid getting tangled up in the canopy. In the distance a waterfall splashed into a massive lake where a sinewy body played in the water. Her mouth hung open as she tried to take it all in.

"It's so beautiful," she breathed. *Beautiful doesn't really cover it, but I don't have the words to describe this.*

Arius gave a satisfied sigh and murmured, "Welcome to my home. Oh, how I've missed this place!"

Sera leant her head against his leg, offering what comfort she could. "Of course, I forgot that it's been decades since you've been here. It truly is an amazing valley, Arius." Reverence coloured her words as she admired his home. "Idyllic. Idyllic is the word I'm looking for."

He released a deep and contented rumble. Heavy wing-beats approached them from behind and they looked up. Arius' father had arrived.

Talegar landed heavily beside them. "You finally made it," he said snidely.

"We got held up," said Arius bitterly.

"What happened?" asked Talegar, tilting his head.

They gave a brief recount of the events leading up to their battle with Desamor at the MRO. Arius slowed his part of the tale and looked to Sera. She cleared her throat. "I am so sorry, Talegar. He wouldn't listen to either of us. He was out for blood. Arius is my Soulbound, I couldn't let him die defending me. So, I entered Desamor's mind and forced him to submit." A sob caught in her throat as her guilt from her actions renewed. "But in doing so, I destroyed his soul. I never meant to!" she cried. "I'm so sorry," she repeated. "But I couldn't bring him back from that." She dashed tears from her cheeks.

Talegar bowed his head for his lost son for only a moment. "Desamor... was always difficult. I will mourn his loss, but I understand that you did what you needed to do."

Sera looked at Arius in shock and projected her thoughts to him. *Why in the Four Gods' names is he being so understanding? He just found out his son is dead!*

*I don't know exactly,* he said slowly. *But my father is always working an angle. He'll use this information to either hold sway over you or get you on his side so he can use your talent against his opponents.*

Talegar raised his head then and continued, "What happened to his body?"

"The IRC took it," said Arius.

"What?" he thundered. "Those brüsjidt!"

Sera looked at Arius in confusion and opened her mind to him.

He noticed her pointed stare and said, *You don't want to know.* At her glare, he relented and answered, *I suppose it's a little like our version of fuck a duck. A profanity. Not a very nice one.*

Sera bobbed her head in understanding but hurried to explain to Talegar what happened during their time in the IRC.

The golden dragon stared at Sera for a long time after she finished her story, making her shift uncomfortably. "So, he is dead then? Not just broken?"

"That's right," she answered, misery saturating her words.

He sent a puff of smoke over her head. "It's for the best. At least your President can't hurt him anymore." He tapped his claws against the earth as he reflected on their journey. "So, then, you successfully linked your mind with Desamor and controlled his body?"

"Yes," she replied warily.

"That is fascinating. What an incredible talent." He was ogling her again.

"I never want to do it again. It was a terrible thing to control someone's free will. So, don't even think about it. I won't be part of any plan you might have where you can use my power for your personal gain."

Talegar had the audacity to look affronted. "I would never! I'm on your side," he purred. "I'd never ask you to do anything you weren't comfortable with."

*Why don't I believe him?* She gave a wry twist of her lips.

*Because he's a liar. And a brüsjidt, but we won't tell him that,* came Arius' snide response.

Sera bit back a snort of laughter. Refocussing on their quest, she said aloud, "I hate to admit it, Talegar," Sera said, "but you were right." Talegar puffed up with self-importance. "The IRC has become corrupted by the humans in power and they've been experimenting on mythics for years. We escaped, but now it's time to put things right. We need to speak to the Elders immediately."

Talegar gave a cutting smile. "I am gratified that you took heed of my warning and have exposed the truth. I will request a Council with the Elders but it may take some time. Dragon Elders live for centuries so nothing can be done in a rush."

Sera narrowed her eyes at the golden dragon and hissed, "We don't have time. Every day more creatures and humans are dying and we have the ability to put an end to it."

Talegar nodded agreeably. "So, it is war then?" he asked.

"No," she replied emphatically. "We don't need another war. We haven't recovered from the Mythic War and neither has dragonkind. We cannot let our pride or our personal beliefs colour our plan. We must come together to forge a peaceful alliance. It's time to review and re-sign the Peace Covenant."

Talegar stilled, aside from a slight flick of the tip of his tail. "I see," he said, his voice devoid of inflection. "I will find the Elders and request an urgent meeting but I cannot promise a timeframe. I will return soon." With that, he leapt from the rocky outcrop and soared away, the sun glistening over his golden scales, almost hurting Sera's eyes.

She released a whoosh of breath that she hadn't realised she'd been holding. "Glad that's over. Now comes the actual hard part," she joked.

# CHAPTER SIXTEEN

"COME," ARIUS MURMURED WITH a nudge of his snout. "Let us bathe and eat to recover from our travels, then we can rest." Together they traipsed through the purple grass. It was springy underfoot and all Sera could imagine was laying down in it and sleeping for an entire day. Shrubs with blue leaves dotted the incline and, as they neared one, a flock of pheasants burst out from their hiding place.

Sera flinched at the birds and giggled nervously. "Sorry, I'm a little on edge still." She cocked her head. "I don't know why but I didn't expect to see something as normal as pheasants in Sky Valley."

Arius gave a throaty chuckle. "What do you think we eat?" he asked her.

She eyed him dubiously. "It seems like you'd need to eat an awful lot of pheasants to fill up. How many pheasants are there?"

His chuckle turned into a booming laugh. "It's not just pheasants, my sweet Soulbound. There are many species of animals that live here. Deer and cattle being the predominant food source. We farm them just as humans do. The dragons in charge of the herds are greatly respected as they manage the sustainability of the animals' numbers. They also tend to the earth on which their herds reside, ensuring that it has the right balance of nutrients to continue stable farming practises into the future."

"Amazing! I had no idea that it would be so... so..." she broke off, looking for the right word that wouldn't cause offence.

"Civilised?" he offered.

She blushed. "Well, yes. It's wonderful."

He huffed a laugh at her pink cheeks.

As they walked down the hill together towards the lake, Sera suddenly noticed the silence. "It's so quiet," she murmured.

Arius gave a dark chuckle. "Indeed, it is. The banished dragon and his pet human have come to the Valley. The Elders haven't given us their blessing, so the dragon community dare not show their support one way or another until they know if we're welcome or not. They'll make themselves scarce until they know the Elders' decision."

"So, dragons don't normally have a differing opinion to those in power then?" She raised an eyebrow.

"I suppose not, no." He returned her look, wondering where she was going with this line of questioning.

"I guess dragonkind isn't that different to humankind after all?"

They'd arrived at the lake now, and Arius slapped his tail into the water, splashing her. "You take that back," he teased.

She giggled and waded in up to her knees. She kicked a spray of water at him. Droplets speckled a tiny patch of his coppery scales and Sera laughed. "No fair. You've got an advantage."

He laughed before launching himself into the lake, disappearing beneath the surface. Quickly removing her jacket, she joined him, relishing the refreshing swim. The temperature was perfect, cold but not freezing. As she stroked over the surface of the lake, the water washed the grime from her clothes.

*I finally feel clean for the first time in... I don't even know how long.*

A chirrup interrupted their fun. Sera spun around to locate the source of the noise and clapped a hand over her mouth. On the bank sat a tiny dragon watching them splashing about in the water.

Eyes shining, she called to Arius, "Look!" and pointed at the bank.

"Don't point, it's rude," he scolded her. "What's the problem? Are you talking about the fledgling?"

"It's a baby dragon, Arius!" she squeaked. Her heart felt fit to burst. The creature was no higher than her knee with indigo feathers covering his body. "It has feathers, too," she exclaimed. "How come?"

Arius chortled. "There are hundreds of species of dragons, majority of which have scales, yes. But there are plenty of the feathered kind, as well. There are also species whose hide are made of diamonds, those who appear to be part of the earth, and others who seem to exist within the very dragonfire we create. I hope to one day show you more of my culture and our history."

Sera gazed in awe at the fledgling. "Is it a boy or a girl?" she asked Arius.

The tiny creature cocked its head at the question in her voice and chirped again.

"This is a young male," he answered. "Maybe a year old. I wonder who his mother is?" He raised his head and combed the tree line.

Sera swam back to shore and waded toward him. The tiny dragon splashed his claws into the water, wanting to join in the fun, but only succeeded in splashing himself in the face. He sat back on the bank with a thud and sneezed. Sera clapped her hands joyfully and burst into peals of laughter.

After wiping the tears of merriment from her eyes, she asked, "Would I be allowed to touch him? Or is that considered rude among your kind?"

"You'd have to request the mother's permission," said Arius, "otherwise you might end up with your hands burnt off." He gave a toothy grin.

Wingbeats sounded above their head and they both looked up to see who Sera could only assume was the mother arriving. She was glorious. The setting sun burnished the stunning cobalt feathers that covered her elegant yet muscular body. She landed and snaked her head forward, her kind azure eyes holding Sera's gaze.

"Greetings, human," said the dragon. "My name is Salixena but you can call me Sally." She turned to Arius. "Young Arius, it has been a long time since I saw your face. I wasn't sure whether I ever would again."

He gave a small bow. "It is good to see you again, Sally. I see your egg has hatched. Congratulations." He walked out of the lake, water glistening on his scales in the afternoon sun.

Sally snorted derisively. "Don't bother with niceties with me, Arius. You have returned to the Valley without a pardon and you've brought a human with you. I can't decide whether you're extremely brave or just plain stupid."

"Let's say a bit of both," he replied with a grin. "But desperate times call for desperate measures. Please allow me to introduce you to my Soulbound."

"Soulbound to a human? How... unorthodox. How did you meet?"

"Seraphina connected telepathically with me by accident so I captured and interrogated her. One thing led to another and we became Soulbound. Later, her memories of me were stripped by her President, but she managed to get them back thanks to a gargoyle's magic. Then, we were captured in the IRC until, with the help of some friends, we managed to escape, blowing half of it up in the process. Now war is coming whether we like it or not unless Sera can convince the citizens of Mandar not to raise their weapons against us."

Sally's jaw dropped and she stared at Arius. "Well, that's a lot to unpack. But I'm going to leave all this talk of war for the Elders to discuss. I need to come back to something you said earlier. You are Soulbound to this human and her name is Seraphina?" she questioned, but there was no judgment in her tone. She was purely asking to clarify the facts.

He nodded an affirmation. "We believe that Sera's great-grandmother was a dragon. We don't yet know whose family she hails from so—"

Sally interrupted with a cry and Sera jumped at the unexpected sound. The blue dragon threw herself to the ground and shoved her face close to Sera's. Sera forced herself to remain still as her heart beat wildly at the sudden proximity of the unfamiliar dragon. "You are my blood, I know it!" she choked out, emotion overflowing in her voice.

"What? Why do you think that?" Sera asked, dumbstruck.

Arius interrupted. "That's right..." he spoke slowly as he pieced it together. "I forgot Sally was related to Seraphina."

"What?" Sera repeated. "I'm so confused. How is Sally related to me?"

Shaking his head, Arius cleared his throat. "I wasn't referring to you. I don't know if you remember, but when you introduced yourself to me, I found your name interesting. That was because there was a dragon named

Seraphina many years ago. She was the Sapphire Dragon in your stories. Tracker Borin and Seraphina were Soulbound and are the only other human-dragon connection I've ever heard of."

"Seraphina was my sister," Sally whispered. "Ever since she disappeared there's been a hole in my heart."

"Disappeared?" Sera demanded. "I thought Hunter Ajax killed the Sapphire Dragon?"

Arius shook his head. "Another lie by your government, I'm afraid."

Rubbing her temples, Sera blew out a frustrated sigh at the new lie she'd uncovered. It felt like the earth was tipping beneath her feet; every time she thought she knew something, another truth would be revealed and she was off-balance again. Opening her mind, Sera studied Sally's aura. It shone a vibrant gold and the edges danced playfully. Upon closer inspection, she noticed the same specks of blue that flecked the aura of her mother's, her nanna's and her own. It was in that moment that she knew it was true. For so long it had just been her and Allen. In the past few months, she'd found out she still had a grandmother, a mother and now a great-great-aunt.

Ignorant to Sera's discovery that their auras looked the same, Sally closed her eyes and scented the air. "I don't know how I know, but I can sense it. She has my sister's blood in her veins." She bugled her joy to the sky before pulling Sera close to her cheek with a wing for a hug. "It is splendid to meet you, niece," Sally whispered, her feathers tickling Sera's cheek.

Sera smiled broadly before burying her fingers into them, running her fingertips over the silky edges. "Did you want me to call you Great-Great-Aunt Sally?"

"Ugh, no, what a horrendous mouthful. And it makes me sound old. Sally is fine."

Realisation dawned on Sera and she turned to look back at the small dragon who had been watching everything with a curious gaze. "And that means you're my cousin, little one."

He bounced up and down happily, fluttering his wings but unable to get airborne. She crouched down and he skipped over to her joyfully.

She glanced at Sally and asked, "Is it okay if I—"

Sally interrupted with a laugh, "Of course! We are family. Corbin, this is your cousin, Seraphina. You look after her."

He shoved his feathery head at her, forcing her to sit, before curling up on top of her crossed legs.

"Oof!" she huffed out. "Hi, Corbin. You're a heavy little guy, aren't you? You're going to grow up big and strong, like your mum." She scratched under his chin as he made happy clicking noises. "Sally..." Sera began. "Would you permit me to connect to your mind?"

The blue dragon gave her a bemused look but shrugged her wings. "Sure."

Sera reached her mind out to Sally's and connected. Sally raised her head abruptly in fear and surprise at the contact.

*It's just me,* said Sera. *Apparently, this is my talent. I can also see the aura of every living thing and I've just begun to sense the feelings of those I connect with. My talent manifested on the night I met Arius, even though I'm a human.*

Sally grinned widely. *Part-human, technically.*

Sera laughed aloud but then grew serious and stared into Sally's eyes. *I don't have the words to explain how this makes me feel. I never knew what I was missing and to find out that I have family, especially of the dragon kind... it feels unbelievable. And yet, it feels so right. Even with all the terrible things that have happened and all the terrible things that might yet come to pass, in this moment, I am so happy. Thank you.*

A contented thrumming rumbled in Sally's chest. Her eyes glimmered with unshed tears. *It is I who should be thanking you. When Seraphina vanished, I too felt alone in the world. It took many years to find a mate and then when we had Corbin, I finally felt whole again. But meeting you now, I— I don't know if I can find the right words either. But my heart feels like it might explode.* She rubbed her feathery cheek against Sera's shoulder. Sera wrapped her arms around her aunt's snout and buried her face into the blue feathers.

*Where is your mate now?*

*Oh, Paoludrin visits every now and then. Dragons don't tend to mate for life unless they become Soulbound. We're still friends and he spends plenty of time with Corbin.*

"That felt bizarre to just sit here and watch while you held a conversation," said Arius. "Now I know how frustrating that must be for others when they're around us, Sera."

She began sniggering but stopped when Sally let out a yelp of astonishment.

Sally sucked in a sharp breath. "I've only just realised... you must be the one they spoke of," she glanced around fearfully and whispered, "in the prophecy."

Arius sidled closer and Sera cocked her head. "People keep mentioning some prophecy but I have no idea if I'm actually the one it refers to or not."

Sally nodded her head eagerly. "You must be! One of the Ancients had a vision many years ago, well before the Mythic War. She's dead now. At the time, we thought it related to the last war, but no one ever showed up who fit the prophecy. The Elders have shared the wording of the prediction with every generation but we'd begun to fear it was just the ramblings of a mad old dragon. The prophecy states:

'Enchanted by lies, abducted for truth,
Blood hid in shadow, hear nature's spirit,
She will break a war, find rebirth in air.'"

"Well, that doesn't make any sense," Sera deadpanned.

"When do prophecies ever make sense?" Arius added with a smirk.

Sally bounced from one talon to another excitedly. "Yes, it does! Think about it! Sera, you had been enchanted by lies from your government your whole life until Arius abducted you and showed you the truth. Your dragon heritage has been hidden from you up until now. And from what you say, you can see creatures' auras when you use your talent."

"And what does the last line mean?"

Sally waved her tail impatiently, as if to sweep Sera's worries away. "I'm still working on that bit, but don't you see? It all fits!"

Sera stopped scratching Corbin's chin and a deep understanding settled into her soul at Sally's reasoning. "You're right, Sally, and it's time we finished fulfilling the prophecy. So, let's go talk to some Elders."

# CHAPTER
# SEVENTEEN

"I LOVE YOUR ENTHUSIASM, Seraphina," Sally said with a grin, "but the Elders won't make a decision without all seven of them present, and Ghalagnur is out on some secret mission. He should be returning to the valley sometime tonight."

Arius' brows lowered in thought as he studied Sera. "Do you know what we can do?" he declared. "While we wait to speak to the Elders, we can tell a story." He inclined his head toward Sera. "Your story."

"My story? What's so special about my story?" Sera asked. "Is it because I'm the 'chosen one?'"

"Oh, my dearest Soulbound. No. It's because of who you are in your heart. You still don't realise how unique you are, even by dragon standards. But the dragons of Sky Valley don't know it yet. And if the Elders turn against us, they will never know it. Come. Let us gather around a bonfire and show our community your kind heart and share your story so they can make up their own minds."

Nodding her head in agreement, Sally rose and said, "Good idea. I'll leave Corbin with you and fetch us some dinner. Take Seraphina to the Gathering Circle and light the torches. I'll meet you there."

With a single bound, Sally threw herself into the air, the backdraft from her wings whipping Sera's hair around her face. After watching Sally disappear behind the tree-tops, the three of them quit the lake with Corbin glued to Sera's side, nudging her hand with his snout.

As they travelled along a path through the dim green light of the forest, Arius leading the way, Sera could feel eyes on her. Every time she looked around to locate the source, all she would find was a rustle of bushes as each dragon hid from her gaze. It made her uncomfortable but she didn't feel threatened.

*I hope Arius is right. I hope they will put aside their fears and come to listen to me. I hope I can convince them I'm worthy of their trust.*

They emerged from the tree line into the half-light of dusk, the purple sky now void of any dragons. A massive open paddock stretched out before them where a herd of deer quietly grazed. The animals seemed unafraid as they walked between the does. No other creatures disturbed the meadow. Arius led them to seven huge boulders arranged in a large circle around a shallow pit. Beside each rock stood a wooden staff with an orange crystal fastened to the top. Sera watched attentively as Arius stopped at each staff, directing a controlled flame at the crystals. As the dragonfire touched each crystal, a garnet-coloured spark ignited inside it, where it grew in intensity. Eventually, the seven crystals were lit, giving off a welcoming glow.

"Why?" Sera asked, waving her hand toward the crystals.

"Tradition," Arius replied simply. "We always light the fire crystals when we meet at the Gathering Circle." Turning away from her, he made his way to the centre of the circle and nudged the ashes in the pit before murmuring, "Time to set the bonfire." He abandoned the circle of light and made his way back to the forest's edge and located a fallen tree. Grasping it in his jaws, he carried it back toward her.

Whilst Corbin didn't speak, he seemed to understand them perfectly. He ran off and found a dried stick in the grass and pranced over to the pit. He threw it on top of Arius' dead tree. He frolicked to the forest and back, bringing a lump of wood each time and adding it to the bonfire.

A joyful roar halted their efforts and they all stared into the sky to find the dragon responsible. "Arius! Sera!" Rainbows danced across the opalescent scales of Aliah as she landed. "What are you doing here, little brother?" She scanned the paddock as she approached. "Do the Elders know? Have you been granted amnesty? Have you returned for good?" she asked hopefully, touching her snout to Arius' forehead in greeting. She mimicked the movement on Sera who caressed her cheek.

"Not yet," Arius replied. "But, don't fear, the Elders know we're here. We await an audience with them. While we're waiting, Sera is going to tell us a story."

"Fabulous!" she crowed. "I look forward to it." Happiness made Aliah's eyes shine as she curled up beside one of the boulders, waiting patiently for Sera to begin.

Arius held his fire until Corbin flumped down beside Sera, then torched the pile of timber. Since the sun had set, a chill had crept into the air, making Sera shiver through her jacket. The newly made campfire offered a soothing warmth and helped to quickly finish drying her damp clothes. Arius lay down and stretched his massive wingspan out, easily fitting between the fire pit and one of the boulders whilst Sera settled in against his foreleg comfortably. Sally arrived soon after and placed two cows and half a dozen pheasants on the ground. Arius grabbed one of the heifers and gobbled it up without ceremony.

Corbin began gnawing on one of the pheasants, sending feathers flying, while Sera began the process of plucking hers.

*I'm not quite ready to eat raw meat just yet, thank you very much.*

She cast around for a green stick to cook it on and Arius said, "Here, allow me to help." He hooked his claw through the inside of the carcass and blew a bubble of fire around it. Sera watched incredulously as he cooked the bird without burning it. The control over his fire magic was awe-inspiring. When he stopped his flames after only ten minutes, Sera raised an eyebrow.

"Will it be cooked all the way through?" she asked. "I don't know if you realise but humans can get food poisoning from undercooked meat."

"Don't worry," he said. "I know how delicate you humans are. It will be cooked through." He offered it to her.

"Hey! You'd better not be calling me delicate." She gave him a playful shove before gratefully accepting the bird, blowing on it to cool the freshly cooked meat.

He chortled. "I'm poking fun at myself too, don't forget," he reminded her. "My human form has the same limitations as yours."

"Really?" she said, as she nibbled her food. "I didn't even think of that. I just figured you'd be able to maintain the same diet in either form."

He shook his head.

Sally rolled her eyes, fluffing her neck feathers in annoyance. "Okay, that's enough talk about food. That's not why we're here."

Sera glanced around at the empty space. "Shouldn't we wait?" she asked. "At least until more dragons arrive to hear what I have to say?"

Sally shook her head. "Speak and they will come." She crossed her forelegs and rested her head on them, the fire glimmering across her feathers. She watched Sera expectantly, who ate her fill before passing the remainder of the pheasant to Arius to finish off.

Corbin burped, a couple of feathers stuck in his teeth, before snuggling up beside Sera. She looked at the four of them — her family — and smiled contentedly.

"I don't really know where to start, but here goes."

# CHAPTER EIGHTEEN

SHE BEGAN AT THE beginning and told how her mother had died when she was only one-year-old, leaving Allen to raise her whilst working full time as a Tracker for the Mythic Relations Office. She spoke of the times she stayed with their family friend, Del, while he was away on the more dangerous missions, and about the times that she was allowed to accompany him on his jobs. She explained how, when she'd finished her secondary schooling, it was a natural progression for her to follow in her father's footsteps so she applied for a Tracker apprenticeship. About how she was an excellent student, yet was shunned by the other apprentices. She spoke of her one close friend Hazel who would do anything for her. How Hazel made life bearable through her education. As she spoke over the crackle of the bonfire, eyes lit up in the darkness surrounding them. Green eyes, yellow eyes, red eyes, each gradually creeping closer to the warm circle of light. Sally was right. As she shared her story, the dragons came to hear her. Tiny, tall, slender, stout, crimson, emerald, feathered and scaled. She smiled at each of the dragons as they entered the Gathering Circle, but continued telling her story. She told them how other mythics integrated into society in Mandar City and how she only tracked the rogue ones; those that had harmed humans or committed crimes. When she mentioned how the taurons that worked in the bank had the company logo branded on their rump, there was a communal hiss of distaste.

One of the smaller red wyverns spoke out then. "That's barbaric," she growled. "They brand their workers?"

Sera frowned as she thought about it and answered slowly. "Only the mythic workers."

There was a general muttering around the fire and Sera cast her mind back. With fresh eyes she could suddenly see all of the other signs of inequality between humans and mythics. The unfairness of it all tore at her heart and she cleared her throat, trying to stomp down the emotion. She explained the, "Capture, don't kill," motto that was drummed into them during training but now realised that it wasn't as sympathetic a motto as she originally thought. They didn't ask them not to kill the mythics out of any kindness for the creatures. It was purely so they could keep the mythics imprisoned in the IRC, harvesting their magic or body parts to create more powerful biological weapons.

She continued on, explaining how she had accidentally connected with Arius' mind and how he'd consequently plucked her from her campsite and stolen her away from everything she knew. She recounted all of the events that had occurred over the previous few weeks, from the President removing her memories of Arius to the discovery that Del was her grandmother but had kept it secret all these years. With tears in her eyes and a lump in her throat, she explained how Desamor's mind was lost. And finally, the revelation that her mother was, in fact, still alive. She went on to tell them how, during her imprisonment, President Kaesus explained how he'd siphoned the magic of many mythics over the years, absorbing portions of their power. When she revealed that the President was her biological father, gasps and snarls rose from the gathered dragons.

One of the green and brown forest dragons raised his head with a snort. His face was covered in bark-like scales and his horns gave the appearance of tree branches. He eyed her distrustfully. "How do we know you're not working for your father and you've come here to take control of our minds?"

There was a ripple of uneasy muttering through the gathered crowd before Arius spoke up, demanding that they quieten down to allow Sera to speak.

"I would be asking the same question in your place," she conceded. "But Arius and I are Soulbound, plus, I discovered I have dragon blood in my veins." There was another surge of murmuring at her revelation. "Unfortunately, I also share blood with that man, but he is not my father. They say you don't get to choose your family, but I refuse to acknowledge him as such. While he held me captive, he insisted I would come to love him as a father, but then he would lash out, cursing me and my love of dragons. I swear, I would never consciously do anything to risk the lives of dragonkind. I left my Personal Security Band and mobile phone behind on purpose so that he couldn't track us here." She stood, pulled back her sleeve and held up her wrist where the obvious tan lines showcased her missing wristband.

In an effort to divert the conversation, Sally piped up and theorised that perhaps the abrupt changes in the President's behaviour were related to his mashup of magic. "Magic is not supposed to be mixed," she explained.

"That would make sense," Sera conceded. Facing the gathered dragons, she spread her hands wide. "I know I'm asking a lot to expect you to trust a human. But I did come here to ask something else of you." More mutters greeted her but Sera forged ahead. "I know I have to speak to your Elders, but I think it's only fair that you know what my journey here was for. I don't want another war. It's the last thing any of us needs. What I want is for a group of dragons—"

"A thunder," Arius whispered in her ear.

"A thunder of dragons to join me and return to Mandar City to show the citizens that they've been lied to by their President. That you aren't extinct and that you pose no threat. I want to show them that we can live in harmony with the mythics but also to show that all magical creatures deserve the same rights as humans." She was shouting by the end of it, trying to be heard over the uproar of all the dragons talking over each other at once.

"Quiet!" roared Arius.

One of the drakes shouted, "You don't get to tell us what to do, banished boy! You have no rights here until the Elders decide your fate."

Arius bared his teeth at the challenge in the drake's voice and stood, towering over the smaller dragon. Sally rose too and herded Corbin away from the confrontation.

Running between them, Sera held her hands up. "Stop! We came here to broker peace between dragons and humans. Not to fight amongst ourselves. Arius is my Soulbound, so don't blame him for being defensive on my behalf. I'm not asking any of you to make a decision right now. I understand we must follow tradition and gain the Elders' approval. I just wanted you to know my story directly from me."

"Yet, you forgot the most important part," came a booming voice from behind Sera.

She jumped and whirled around, her mouth hanging open as the hill came to life. What she had thought was a slope leading toward the forest, was, in fact, an enormous dragon. Her heart beat wildly and adrenaline coursed through her body as he separated himself from the earth. Eyes darting, Sera struggled to absorb the colossal mythic. She realised now his body was covered in short green fur that looked like grass, helping him blend in. Moss hung from his jaw and his horns looked like jagged boulders. *I still don't understand how I didn't notice him when we arrived.*

Sally beamed at the dragon. "Welcome back, Ghalagnur. You do love to make an entrance."

The stranger loosed a rumbling laugh that echoed over the valley. "That's a fair observation." He turned to Sera and added as an aside, "Don't feel badly for not noticing me. My talent is camouflage. And, being as large as I am, it is certainly a boon when I want to spy."

Lowering his head to be on the same level as Sera, Arius whispered, "Ghalagnur is the Elder we were waiting on."

Sera gave an almost imperceptible nod as she stared at the beast, wrestling with her terror.

Raising his head to four times the height of Arius, Ghalagnur announced to the gathered thunder, "Seraphina Azura is the one we have been waiting for these many years.

'Enchanted by lies, abducted for truth,
Blood hid in shadow, hear nature's spirit,
She will break a war, find rebirth in air.'

The prophecy has finally come to pass." He trumpeted a roar that reverberated through Sera's bones, forcing her to her knees.

At his call, six other dragons flew swiftly from the darkness and landed on the boulders around the pit, Talegar among them. Ghalagnur was the largest and rested his front talons on his boulder. Meanwhile, the smallest of the Elders, a miniature amphiptere, perched on the very tip of her boulder, her scarlet wings tucked in close to her serpentine body. The rest of the dragons quietened and backed away from the Gathering Circle, offering their respect to the Elders.

The tiny amphiptere spoke then, her steely eyes examining Sera carefully, "Talegar tells us you have requested an audience. I assume that Arius wishes to lift his banishment, but what in the Four Gods names would a human want with the Elders?"

Ghalagnur replied on Sera's behalf, "She is the one we've been waiting for."

"Ghal! Shut your mouth for a moment, please," snapped the diminutive dragon. "I asked the human."

Blood rushing in her ears, she pushed down the spike of fear that threatened to overwhelm her as seven Elders scrutinised her. With a wavering voice, Sera announced, "I am the great-granddaughter of Seraphina, the Sapphire Dragon. And I come before you to beg for your support."

# CHAPTER NINETEEN

WITH THE BACKING OF Arius, Aliah, Sally and Talegar, along with the frequent interruptions of support from Ghalagnur, it hadn't taken long for the Elders to deliberate over their fate. Arius' banishment was lifted in short order and, upon hearing Sally's analysis of the prophecy, they agreed to send a thunder of dragons to Mandar City as witnesses. They would go there to support Sera's request to amend and re-sign the Peace Covenant. The rest of the able-bodied dragons would be on standby to attack if Kaesus refused to back down. If the thunder hadn't returned within three days, they would fly on Mandar City. Aliah, Sally and Ghalagnur volunteered immediately. They opened up the offer to the other dragons assembled around the Gathering Circle. The amphiptere Elder, whose name, Sera found out, was Vera, also stepped up.

Before anyone else could put their name forward, Vera announced, "Seven. Seven is a number of power. So it is the number of Elders, and so it shall be the number of this fellowship."

A green wyvern named Wuranax and a cream dragon name Lylerion came forward. Including Arius, that made seven dragons. Their thunder was complete.

"Get some rest," Vera commanded. "We leave at first light."

The dragons slowly dispersed leaving Sera alone with her family.

"Will you stay with us tonight?" asked Sally. Corbin frolicked around Sera, making her decision easy.

"Of course!" Sera said, before ruffling the feathers atop her cousin's head. He chirruped joyfully.

"You'll join us, won't you Aliah?" asked Sally.

"I'd love to," she replied with a beaming smile.

Since he couldn't fly by himself yet, Sally picked up Corbin in a talon and took to the air, followed closely by Aliah. Sera clambered aboard Arius and they trailed after them. Arius' wingbeats were slow and he didn't speak.

"You seem troubled. What's wrong?" Sera asked softly.

"I was just thinking... I hope you don't regret meeting me. It's my fault that you've been dragged into this predicament. Torn from your comfortable life, thrown into a conflict that wasn't yours, convincing mythics you thought were extinct to fight a battle you've only been embroiled in because of me... I feel guilty. It's my fault you're here."

She smacked his shoulder. "Don't! If I could go back," she said, "I wouldn't change a thing about what happened. If you hadn't taken me, I wouldn't be here. Because of you, I found out my mother is still alive. Because of you, I've met my aunt and cousin. Because of you, I want to be a better person. Never apologise for that."

He turned his head to study her briefly before facing forward once more. "Are you sure? You're not just saying that to protect my feelings?"

She rolled her eyes. "I'm not as overprotective as you. So, no, I'm not sparing your feelings."

He grunted at her dig but didn't respond.

Sera wished she could prod him a little longer to draw out a smile but they had already arrived at Sally's cave in the mountainside. As soon as they landed and Sera dismounted, Corbin was on her. He gently took her hand in his jaw and tugged her toward the side of the cave. It wasn't a simple cave though. The stalagmites had been melted together to form partitions between the areas. Corbin was leading her around one of the stone walls to his version of a bedroom. He had a festive-looking nest, filled with colourful leaves and flowers. Some were dried and faded whilst others had obviously only been placed there that day. He released her hand and trilled sharply, pointing his snout toward a corner of his nest. Sera hung over the side of the nest and searched for whatever it was he was so keen to show her. A yellow moth, larger than her hand, fluttered out, making her leap back in surprise. It flitted to Corbin's head and landed, waving its antenna toward her. The fledgling bounced on the spot, chirping happily.

"Is that your friend?" she asked, bemused. He nodded enthusiastically, the moth sticking like glue through its wild ride. "I see. He's lovely. Thank you for introducing us."

Corbin trilled again and the moth flew back to its spot in his nest. He led the way back to the main living area where they'd landed and curled up in front of the fire Sally had set. Aliah and Arius were deep in conversation near the cave entrance while Sally had disappeared behind one of the stone partitions to prepare a nest for Arius and Sera to share. The light of the flames danced over the cave walls, throwing bizarre shadows and making Sera blink. Not wanting to interrupt the siblings, she sat cross-legged beside Corbin and began running her fingertips over the feathers behind his ear. He made a noise that sounded very much like a purr and leaned into her hand. Then sniffed, the skin around his nose wrinkling.

And sniffed again. He raised his head and held a strange expression before giving an enormous sneeze. A small stream of fire escaped his mouth at the same time and lit her grey pants on fire. She yelped and leapt up, smacking at the flames until they died. Corbin whined and sniffed her tattered clothing before dropping his head in shame.

"Are you all right?" Arius demanded, shoving his head forward and sniffing her leg.

"Yeah, I'm fine," she said, puzzled by his excessive concern.

"Dragonfire is fiercer than standard fire and has magical properties, meaning it causes major damage to human skin. Even though Corbin is only a fledgling, I still would have expected there to be at least a small burn." He eyed her unmarked skin dubiously.

The musical voice of Aliah gently reminded them, "She is part-dragon. Perhaps her blood offers her some protection from our fire the same way ours does?"

With another whine, Corbin bunted her thigh apologetically.

Sera laughed. "Don't fret, little man, I'm fine. And I didn't like these clothes anyway."

Sally appeared from behind one of the walls then, holding something in her foretalon and said, "Perfect timing, son. I figured you'd want to get out of that disgusting uniform as soon as possible, Sera. Here, I have garments for you both." She placed a pile of fabric between Sera and Arius.

He transformed into his human form, still wearing the boxy gown from the IRC.

"I don't think I realised that you kept your clothes on from your last change," Sera said, tilting her head as she considered his magic. "I guess I assumed you always changed into the same outfit."

Arius nodded matter-of-factly. "Whatever I was wearing before I last shifted back to my natural form, is what I will be wearing next time I transform into a human again."

The other dragons turned their heads away to offer some privacy as Arius pulled the gown over his head and began pulling on the black trousers that were in the pile. Sera eyed his tanned body, admiring the muscles as they stretched and bunched. He saw her watching and smirked, but said nothing.

Shaking her head to rid her mind of the lascivious thoughts that were flooding it, Sera cleared her throat and asked Sally, "Where did you get the pants from?"

"Funny story, actually. Last time Paoludrin left the valley, he ran into a black lynx who gave them to him. He had no need for them but didn't want to offend the mythic by refusing his gift so brought it back here for Corbin to play with."

Arius and Sera shared a look. "That cat!" Arius exclaimed as Sera chuckled. "He even brought the right size. Incredible."

Sera picked up the second garment and held it up. The dark blue fabric shimmered and slid through her fingers like liquid. It was Arius' turn to watch her with hooded eyes as she peeled the IRC uniform from her body. She gave him a mischievous wink before slipping into the full-length bodysuit. It fit her perfectly, almost seeming to mould to her body. She reached her arms above her head, pleased to find the clothes allowed her to fully stretch out without hindering her movements.

"This is amazing. Did Idris give this to your mate as well?"

Sally looked back toward the fire now that the humans were dressed. "Idris? Oh, the lynx. No, actually. They belonged to Seraphina. My sister's talent was the same as yours, Arius."

"She could turn into a human?" Sera clarified. At Sally's nod, she said, "That explains a few things." Throwing her stolen IRC uniform into the fire, she watched it burn with a grim satisfaction before adding, "Thank you for the clothes, Sally." Looking to her aunt with a grin, her lips fell when she realised Sally was crying. "What's the matter? Did I say something wrong?" She shot Arius a panicked look but he shrugged, at a loss as to why the blue dragon had tears rolling over her feathered cheeks.

"No," she sniffed, "it's just... seeing my sister's clothes being worn again... it's nice. But, also hard. I miss her. The not-knowing is the hardest. I'm certain that she's still alive, but why didn't she return to Sky Valley? Why didn't she come back to me?" She buried her face beneath a wing while she sobbed.

"Oh, Sally. I'm so sorry."

"It's not your fault," she replied, her voice muffled by the feathers.

Sera closed the gap between them and leant her head against Sally's shoulder. "I'm sorry that it hurts. I'm sorry that you lost your sister. I wish I could make it better. But I can't. And that sucks. But we will remember her. Once all this is over, I'd love to stay with you for a while and learn all about her."

"I'd like that," she hiccoughed, peeking out from under her wing, her eyes shining with gratitude.

"Speaking of apologies, there's one I haven't made yet," Sera said, wincing at the news she was about to deliver to the most sweet-tempered dragon she'd ever met. She blew out a long breath, steeling herself but before she could begin, Aliah interrupted her.

"If this is about Desamor, there is no need to apologise," Aliah said, snaking her head closer to Sera.

Arius slipped his arm around Sera's waist and whispered, "I've already told her everything."

"But Aliah... it's all my fault. Did Arius explain that I broke Desamor's mind when I took control? If I hadn't done that, Kaesus wouldn't have been able to use his body in the battle at the IRC and he wouldn't have died." Sera hung her head, guilt wrapping its sickly tendrils around her heart and squeezing tightly. "It's my fault that your brother is dead," she whispered.

Arius tried to pull her in for a hug but she pushed him away, angry tears beginning to spill.

"Don't," cooed Aliah, tipping Sera's chin up with a talon to meet her earnest gaze. "It was a terrible accident. I know you never meant to hurt anyone. The way I see it, if you hadn't taken control of Desamor, I would be grieving for a different brother."

The dragon's gentle words broke through the fog of shame that had descended upon Sera. Her shoulders slumped and she sucked in a shaking breath. "I... I know that. But I still feel awful about what happened. I'm so scared that I'll accidentally end up like my biological father. He does whatever he needs to do to get what he wants. I never want to be like him."

"And you won't, Sera," said Aliah firmly. "I know it in my wings."

Sally nodded emphatically from where she sat at the edge of the firelight, listening to their exchange.

Once again, Arius gently tugged her into his embrace; this time she let him. "The Gods chose you to be my Soulbound," he said. "I don't think you can get a higher vote of confidence."

Sera smiled into his chest and nodded, accepting his love and Aliah's acceptance. Turning her head away from the tickle of his chest hairs, she said to Aliah, "Thank you for understanding. Just know that I am sincerely sorry for your loss."

Sally wrapped a feathery wing around the opalescent dragon, offering her comfort. Aliah bowed her head, sorrow marring her features. "I will grieve for the fledgling that I used to play with. Desamor was a happy baby but he changed as he grew up. Then, after we lost our mother, he embraced the darkness. I couldn't find a way to bring him back into the light. He would have destroyed himself one way or another." With a sigh, Aliah rose and announced, "I will take my leave now. I'll see you at sunrise."

After saying their farewells, she leapt from the cave entrance, disappearing quickly into the night. They all agreed then that it was time to sleep and gather their energy in preparation for the long flight ahead. Sally picked up a sleeping Corbin and placed him gently on his nest before retiring to her own.

Sera lay on her back and stared at the ceiling. As the night deepened and the fire burned low, she admired the beauty of the glow worms that lit up the ceiling of the cave. Soft snores from Corbin echoed through the space, bringing a smile to her lips. Surrounded by her loved ones, her heart felt full. Everything was going to plan.

# CHAPTER TWENTY

THE NIGHT BEGAN RECEDING, the sun threatening to arrive at any moment as the three dragons and Sera wolfed down a light breakfast. Flying to the flat ground at the base of the mountain, they walked through the forest, following a trail large enough for two dragons to walk abreast. As the sky brightened, filtering soft light through the canopy, the forest began to wake, birdsong and insects singing their morning salutations. They stopped at the lake briefly and refilled Sera's water bottles. She stored them in her backpack and slung it over her shoulders. Corbin frolicked around them, stretching his legs and fluttering his wings furiously in an attempt to get airborne. Arius offered her a comforting nudge with his snout but didn't say anything. As a family unit, they marched toward the Gathering Circle. The seven Elders gathered in a semi-circle, Talegar among them. The rest of the field was filled with dragons of all sizes milling about, come to bid their friends goodbye and watch the momentous event. Sally hung back to give Corbin over to his father. Paoludrin would be caring for the fledgling while she was away bearing witness to Sera's peace offering. Arius and Sera stopped in front of the Elders and bowed their heads in a respectful greeting, but remained silent.

Talegar opened his mouth to say something but Vera flew in front of his face and cut him off. "No time for niceties, we've got to go," she shouted.

Sera caught a brief look of fury cross the gold dragon's face but he quickly schooled his features into a blank slate. "Fly fierce, my son," he said to Arius. "I pray to Caehli for your success."

Arius bobbed his head and gave the expected reply. "Strike strong, father." He turned his back on his father and Sera saw Talegar's tail twitch in annoyance.

*I still don't trust your father.*

*That's very wise. Here's hoping he hasn't murdered the other Elders by the time we return.* Arius' tone was joking, but she sensed an undercurrent of worry as he considered the possibility.

She placed a pacifying hand against his scales. *That's a problem for another day. There's no use worrying about it now.*

*You're right, of course.* He dropped to the ground, waiting for her to mount. *Ready to fly?*

*Always.* She clambered up his side, settling into the place she now called her spot, and adjusted the position of her backpack to be more comfortable.

Vera flitted onto Ghalagnur's shoulder in preparation for take-off. Her diminutive size meant she wouldn't be able to keep up with the group, so Ghal had offered to carry her. The enormous dragon roared, making Sera's teeth rattle. At his cue, the seven dragons who had volunteered took to the skies, their wings pumping hard. The sound of their wingbeats crafted a pulsing beat that filled Sera's very being.

*Now I know why it's called a thunder.*

She gazed around at the seven dragons. Her heart beat joyfully at the sight. For the first time in decades, a thunder of dragons abandoned Sky Valley to wing its way toward Mandar City.

It had been a tiring journey. They hadn't spoken much, only focusing on their flight. One by one, the dragons landed gratefully on the clifftops overlooking the Kaldern Ocean.

Arius announced to the thunder, "We will hunt and rest, then advise our allies of our arrival."

Wuranax and Lylerion leapt off the cliff to hunt sea creatures. Sera heard them chatting to one another about the difference in taste between freshwater and saltwater prey. Ghal quickly set a bonfire going and Sally laid down to recover, her body not used to long flights. Aliah joined her and asked about Corbin, receiving an animated response and successfully distracting the mother from her aching muscles. Throughout their journey, Sera had been thrilled to find that her great-grandmother's bodysuit adjusted well to the various temperatures. It had kept her warm through the windy flight and, now that the afternoon sun was heating her back, it kept her cool.

Vera flapped her wings and flew up to land on Sera's shoulder. The crimson Elder's serpentine body was far colder than Arius', making Sera wonder whether she could breathe fire. Vera asked, "How will we let your friends know that we're here? We have no way of communicating with them."

Sera gritted her teeth in frustration. "If only I had my phone. I could call Hazel and ask her to find Wren or Helena who could get in touch with the Little Birds for us. And then we need to figure out how to arrange the meeting with Kaesus."

Arius suggested, "I can shift into my human form and sneak into the city. I'm not quite as recognisable as you, Sera, so I'll have less chance of being identified."

"No way," exclaimed Sera. "I won't let you risk yourself like that. The President knows what you look like and is bound to have plastered photos of your face all over the city. And if you go anywhere near him, he'll capture you before you can say 'Caehli.'"

"I could camouflage myself and sneak in," suggested Ghalagnur.

"Gods!" Vera winced. "Volume, Ghal!" Sera eyed the giant dragon dubiously. Before she could voice her concerns, Vera rolled her eyes and added, "You're a very sweet, but very stupid dragon."

He looked affronted at her insult. "Don't call me stupid. My talent is to blend in, I'm the perfect candidate for the job."

"Yes," she spoke slowly, as if to a child, "and you're excellent at pretending to be a hill. But this is a city. I think people will notice if a hill pops up overnight."

Ghalagnur grumbled darkly while Sera covered up her giggle with a cough.

Another voice prickled at the edge of Sera's mind and said, *I'll do it.*

With the voice having been projected to all four of them, Vera, Arius, Ghal and Sera all snapped their heads around towards the edge of the forest.

"Idris?" Sera asked aloud.

"And this is why I don't tell people about my abilities." The lynx appeared from the shadows of the canopy and jumped onto the ground, stalking towards them. He gave a long-suffering sigh. "Where's the mystery? Where's the intrigue? It's so much more fun when I have secrets," he pouted.

"How did you know we'd be here?" asked Sera.

"Nope. Nuh-uh. No way. I get to keep one secret, thank you very much." His tail curled, the flame at the tip flaring in his annoyance. "I couldn't help overhearing your earlier discussion. No one recognised me during the battle at the IRC and I'm good at blending in," he said. "Allow me to travel into the city on your behalf. Who would you like me to contact and what message shall I pass along?"

The dragons shared a look before Arius gave Idris a formal reply. "An excellent notion. The dragons offer you our thanks. Sera?" he deferred to her. "What message would you like Idris to give and to whom?"

"We need to tell the Little Birds that the dragons are going to reveal themselves to the world tomorrow. As far as anyone knew, they were extinct until Desamor and Arius showed up. We need to let them know that there's a whole society of your kind waiting to peacefully reintegrate with society. Our primary objective is to amend and re-sign the Peace Covenant with changes that allow mythics the same rights as humans. The citizens of Mandar need to be told about the harvesting of mythics so it never happens again. Obviously, amending the Covenant will be a long process in itself but if we can establish a truce, we can start working together. We want the Little Birds to act as witnesses to our request to amend the treaty. We also want fighters present as back-up, should the talks go sour."

Idris nodded along with her requests. "A solid plan," he agreed. "Anything else?"

"Please ask Urma to get a message to President Kaesus. Tell him his Little Blue Bird wants to talk. We will meet him at midday tomorrow. We'll need the meeting in a neutral space where the dragons have room to land, and fight if necessary, so I suggest we meet in the fourth quadrant of the fallow fields, east of the city. Lastly, tell the Little Birds to get a message out to all the citizens of Mandar City. Tell them, if they want to see the President's lies exposed, to come to the meadow at noon."

"Excellent," purred Idris. "I will deliver your messages and see you tomorrow."

Sera knelt in front of the big cat and cupped his cheeks in her hands, careful to avoid the black flames licking his spine and neck. "Thank you for everything, Idris. I know how much you love your snark and cryptic advice. But I also know that you're a big softy under all of that. I want you to know that I'm glad to call you my friend."

A purr rumbled deep in his chest and he pushed his wet nose into her cheek. "And I you, Seraphina. I look forward to embracing the new world you will herald in for all of us."

Incredulous, Sera gawked at him. "I think that's one of the least mysterious and nicest things you've ever said to me."

# CHAPTER TWENTY-ONE

THE SUN HAD BEGUN its slow descent toward the mountains at her back as Sera picked her way carefully down the narrow track on the side of the cliff. The salty spray of the ocean that was carried by the easterly wind caressed her cheeks. Idris had left to deliver her messages, and most of the dragons were either eating or sleeping. Panting slightly, Sera arrived safely on the shore and proceeded to fill her empty water bottle up with sea water. She didn't really need to replenish it since she'd only just filled them that morning, but she felt the need to do something with her hands. Helplessness harried the edge of her thoughts, and, if she gave in to it, she worried she wouldn't be able to pull herself out again. Pulling out the Filter tonic from her backpack, she methodically measured and added it to her canteen. It would extract the salt and bacteria, leaving it as drinkable fresh water. A small smile played across her lips as she studied the rock pools, remembering the last time she'd been here with Balthazar and fought the scorpius. Her brows pulled down and her smile dropped as she recalled the empty shell she saw at the IRC.

Arius landed beside her and quickly transformed into a human, remaining shirtless, with only his trousers to cover his lower half. His soft voice interrupted her melancholy thoughts. "Why are you sad, my dear Seraphina?" He slid an arm around her shoulders.

"Just remembering all the terrible things I've acciden-tally been a part of, because I didn't know any better." She gestured at the closest rock pool. "I fought a scorpius here once and immobilised it. I called the MRO to advise that the mythic had attacked me. I figured they'd tag it, measure it and re-release it into a less populated area. It's not like scorpius can be taught right from wrong. I never knew until recently, but when the MRO picked it up, they took it to the IRC, killed it and used its body for parts. I saw the empty shell when I was in there." She shuddered, feeling ill. "And now I wonder how many of my other missions were falsified? Like that snow foxen that killed a child. Did it really? I never heard anything on the news. What if I helped lay the trap for that poor creature when it had done nothing wrong? Everything I've ever worked towards has come into question and it makes me sick."

The gentle ocean breeze pulled a few wisps of her hair around to tickle her face. Arius ensnared the auburn strands with his fingers and tucked them behind her ear. "It's a terrible thing the MRO and IRC have done. I don't have any words to make it better. Just know that it's not your fault. You never meant any ill will."

"That's true," Sera sighed, "but still..." she trailed off, looking out at the Kaldern Ocean, the peaceful symphony of the waves at odds with the turmoil in her heart.

Arius pulled her in to his body, tucking her head under his chin. "But still," he echoed, offering what comfort he could.

With her ear pressed against his skin, she could hear his heart beating steadily in his chest. "I'm scared," she whispered. "What if everything goes wrong tomorrow?"

Arius didn't have an answer for her. He grasped her chin with his hand and tipped her face up to his, covering her mouth with his lips. The sun disappeared and left behind a stunning display of purples, pinks and oranges but Sera and Arius didn't notice. As their kiss intensified, he lifted her up, wrapping her legs around his hips, and carried her across the rocks, before laying her down in the sand. His lips left hers and began exploring her jawline, before trailing down her neck. She moaned at the fire burning across her body from his touch. He deftly removed her bodysuit before letting his hands stroke every inch of her skin, each touch a tender caress. The scent of embers and spice tickled her nose and sweat beaded on her temple as he explored her body. She trembled beneath him as she traced his shoulders with her fingertips, following the lines of muscle down his torso.

He groaned and leant his forehead against hers. "Gods, but this is intense in this form," he muttered.

She granted him a smile filled with love. "I'll try to be gentle with you," she teased before tugging impatiently at his pants.

He chuckled at her antics before his emerald eyes turned serious. "Are you sure you want this? I don't want you to feel pressured."

"You're very sweet to ask." She trailed her fingertips down his arms as she thought about how to answer. "I don't know what awaits us tomorrow. I don't really want to think about it right now. What I do know is that I don't want to waste this moment. All I want is you." She stroked his cheek. "All of you." She waited impatiently as he undid the button on his pants, before tugging them off and throwing them to the side. He settled his naked body between her hips and waited for her to guide him forward. They held each other's gazes as they joined their bodies, riding their pleasure into the night.

# CHAPTER TWENTY-TWO

THE NEXT MORNING, THE dragons and Sera arranged themselves in various positions of repose on the top of the cliff. She'd tossed and turned all night. It felt like déjà vu from her original meeting with Talegar to decide whether she was dangerous. But this time, the meeting wouldn't just decide whether she lived or died. It would determine the future of the mythic species. As the sun rose slowly above the ocean, they passed the time by eating until their bellies were full and sharing happy stories of the past. Their joyful tales of growing up in Sky Valley filled Sera with wonder. The mood was light-hearted and frivolous as they each tried to ignore the undercurrent of fear for what the day would bring.

Sera yawned, then sluggishly stood up and stretched. "I miss coffee," she complained to herself before running her hands over her hair in a vain attempt to flatten the flyaway mess. The sand that had worked itself into her scalp yesterday certainly hadn't helped matters. With a defeated sigh, she gave up, resigned to looking like a fluffy-haired clown.

"Come here, niece," Sally curled a talon around her torso and pulled her close. "I've seen you patting your tangled nest the whole trip. Let me fix it for you."

Sera burst out laughing. "And how, exactly, do you plan on doing that, aunt? Have you been hiding a hairbrush under those feathers? Although, I think we're past the abilities of a hairbrush now. Maybe we need some scissors?"

The exposed blue skin around Sally's eyes crinkled as she smiled secretively. "No scissors needed, Sera. I will, of course, be using my talent," she whispered. Before Sera could ask what her talent was, she touched the tip of her nose to the top of Sera's head and a rush of warmth tingled through her scalp. Sera shivered at the unexpected sensation and raised her hands to her hair. Her locks fell in silky waves over her shoulders, no sign of a single knot to be found.

Sera's mouth fell open. "How?" she exclaimed.

"My talent is rather obscure. I have the ability to fix that which is broken. But it's a weak version. I can fix the nest in your hair without much effort. But ask me to repair a broken leg and I'll need a week to recover my strength. And it only works on physical things. I can't fix a broken heart, for example."

"That's fantastic!" Sera clapped her hands in amazement.

Sally preened at the compliment. "It's certainly been handy with young Corbin. Children tend to break things. How do you think your great-grandmother's clothes were still in such good condition? I can't even tell you how many things Corbin has burnt in the last year."

"Not that I cared about the uniform, but why didn't you just fix my clothes when Corbin burnt them?"

Sally gave a derisive sniff. "Well, you didn't really want to continue to wear a uniform from the IRC, did you? Plus, it gave me the opportunity to see my sister's clothes being used again. Which has been utterly delightful." Gazing at Sera, her azure eyes warmed before growing distant at some treasured memory. She shook her feathered head to pull herself back into the present.

The sound of distant hoofbeats put them all on high alert and Sera quickly pulled Firinne out of its sheath whilst casting her mind into the forest. She relaxed her stance and her eyebrows rose in surprise. "It's Balthazar. With... Hazel?"

It didn't take long for the buckskin stallion to burst out onto the open clifftop. He slid to a stop and reared in shock at the sight of the seven dragons observing their arrival. Hazel threw herself onto his neck and frantically scrambled to grab some mane to avoid falling off. He returned to the earth and muttered a quick apology to her.

She dismounted, awkwardly sliding off Balthazar's side and landing on shaking legs.

Sera rushed forward and wrapped her up in a tight hug. "Hazel! Balthazar! What in Ghaia's name are you both doing here? Are you okay? Why did you come?"

Tears were streaking down Hazel's face as she gasped out, "I'm sorry, Sera. Your friend, Idris, he's gone."

Sera grasped the tops of Hazel's arms and stared into her eyes. "Gone? What do you mean gone?"

"I mean, he's dead!" she cried, her voice breaking on the dreaded word.

"How?" Sera demanded.

"He saved me," she wailed, "but he got shot in the process."

Sera ground out, "Who shot him?"

"The Director."

"What?" Sera asked, taken aback. "I don't understand. Start at the beginning."

Balthazar touched his horn to Hazel's shoulder, the stones surrounding the base flashing briefly. Her sobs eased and she took some steadying breaths while Sera passed her a water bottle. Hazel swigged a few mouthfuls, then wiped her face on her shirt collar. Sera sat her down on the ground and rubbed her back while she waited for her friend to explain.

"While you were gone, I joined the Little Birds. Wren recognised me from seeing us together in Tregua Park so told me to follow him. That stupid werewolf nearly squashed me when I arrived at the new nest but luckily Tracker Helena was there to vouch for me. They've moved their headquarters since their last one was discovered by the President. This morning, I was walking toward their new location. I was trying so hard to remain vigilant, like they told me, when I noticed someone tailing me. I was trying to shake them when I ran into your lynx. He took one sniff and recognised me as your friend. He introduced himself and told me you were out here on the cliffs, but the whole time he seemed agitated. His flames kept flaring and he couldn't stand still. He asked me to tell you that your messages to the Little Birds and the President had been delivered. When I asked him why he couldn't tell you himself, he gave me a sad smile and—" she began weeping again, "—he leapt in front of me right when my pursuer pulled the trigger. He was alive, and then he wasn't. I didn't know what to do. I'm not trained to handle that kind of thing like you are. The man came closer, looked at Idris, then at me, shrugged and said, 'That works.' That was when I realised it was the Director of the MRO. I accused him of murder and he just told me to pass a message on to you. He said, 'The President accepts your invitation and looks forward to meeting his Little Blue Bird and her flock at noon.' And then he just walked away. He just walked away, like none of it mattered. And all I did was stand there, shaking."

"I was returning from a meeting with the Little Birds and found her like that," Balthazar murmured. "I managed to get enough sense out of her to bring her here."

"So, the Director is working for the President, then." Sera stood up and began pacing back and forth in front of Hazel, fury pounding through her entire being. She wanted to throw every curse word under the sun but knew it wouldn't bring Idris back.

Arius watched her warily, unfamiliar with how to deal with her rage, and sent waves of calming energy through their bond. "The President would have ordered the hit on your friend to make you angry," he said.

"Yeah, well, it's fucking working," she spat out, ignoring his power. "They all deserve to die for this. First Tormund, then Aaron, now Idris? And that's not including the countless other innocents who have been murdered over the years."

Arius continued, trying to reason with her, "If they take away someone you care about, you'll lose your temper and lash out. When you lose control of your emotions, you make mistakes."

"Don't give into it," murmured Sally.

Aliah added quietly, "Desamor did, and look where that got him."

That made Sera pause.

Arius saw her hesitation and forged ahead, "If you arrive in Mandar City, having promised the citizens you're there to welcome in a new age of peace, and then immediately attack the President without obvious provocation, the people won't see you as a saviour. All they'll see is a monster. Don't give in to your rage, Seraphina. If you do, you'll be just like them. And that's not who you are. Idris didn't sacrifice himself for you to throw it all away. He knew you were better than that." He transformed into a human and held his palm up, showing her his golden scar from when they became Soulbound. He pressed it over her heart, where her matching scar sat. "Come back to me, my Soulbound. I understand your feelings. I am angry, too. I know you are lost in your grief right now, but do not let it consume you." He leant his forehead against hers and whispered, "Come back to me."

She squeezed her eyes closed and trembled at the tumult of emotions swirling inside her. She knew Arius was right. They all were. On instinct, she opened her mind to the world around her. The outpouring of love and concern shone through the auras of the gathered dragons. The strength of their emotions nearly dropped her to her knees. These dragons barely knew her but had abandoned their home and followed her to pave the way to a new world. She refused to mar Idris' memory by ruining all their hard work.

Taking a deep, shuddering breath, she opened her eyes and stared into the earnest green gaze of Arius. She rasped out, "I'm okay now. You're right, of course. I was just... so angry. But I won't let it control me."

"That's my girl." Holding her tightly, Arius kissed her tenderly. Drawing away, his emerald eyes still locked on hers, he said, "I don't know if I ever told you, but it was Idris who advised me to seek you out." He snorted. "Not in so many words, of course. That lynx did like to keep things cryptic. But he told me that something I was seeking would be in the Mandar ranges on the night that I found you. He was a wily one, wasn't he? Always seemed to be one step ahead."

She gave a half-choked sob. "Yes, he was a clever cat. And we were lucky to have him on our side."

They held each other for a long time, leaning on one another to hold them up in their grief. Eventually, she extricated herself from his arms and turned to her friends. After offering her thanks to Balthazar and giving him a scratch on his chest — his favourite spot — she helped Hazel to her feet. "Are you feeling okay now?" Sera asked her.

"Kind of feel like I should be asking you the same question," Hazel muttered with a sideways look. Arius snorted at their banter and returned to his dragon form. "Woah," Hazel breathed in awe at the transformation.

Ignoring her Soulbound's exhibitionism, Sera grabbed her friend in another tight hug. "I'll be okay. Thank you for finding us so we could hear what happened to Idris directly from you. I wish you weren't involved in any of this so I'd know that at least one of my friends were safe. And far away from any potential battles. But I must admit, it makes me so happy to see you."

"I'm glad to see you safe, too." Hazel squeezed her back before looking up at the dragon. "Hey, Arius. Nice to finally see you in your natural form."

Arius brought his head low to look Hazel in the eye. "You have a brave heart. Your Perry chose wisely when he picked you."

"But I rescued him?"

"He lets you think that. But cats are always the ones doing the choosing."

# CHAPTER TWENTY-THREE

IT WASN'T LONG BEFORE Balthazar was nudging Hazel with his muzzle, indicating it was time for them to go. "If you want us on the field at noon," he said to Sera, "we need to leave now."

Sera gave Hazel a leg up into the saddle before giving Balthazar a scratch on the wither. "We'll be okay," she insisted, pasting on a smile that didn't quite reach her eyes.

Hazel reached forward and disrupted her scratching to squeeze Sera's hand. "I know."

With a wave from Hazel and a snort from the unicorn, they plunged back into the forest. Since it would only take fifteen minutes as the dragon flies to get from the clifftops to the meeting place, the thunder had decided to hang back to avoid an early arrival. The next hour seemed to drag on for eternity. Sally, Aliah, Arius and Sera stayed on the cliffs, while Ghalagnur went off to hunt again, with Vera accompanying him. The giant dragon needed to consume vast amounts of meat to keep his energy up. Wuranax was flying the perimeter of their camp to watch for spies, while Lylerion had flown ahead to scout the surrounds of the field to ensure the President's forces weren't laying any traps. He promised to meet up with them before they arrived at the field.

Sera groaned at the inaction. *Waiting on the precipice of the moment when either peace wins or a war breaks out is worse than death. Probably. Not that I would know how death feels. But anything is better than this.* To keep her hands busy, she pulled out Firinne and examined the blade. Its edge was a little dull and the runes weren't as clear as they used to be. She frowned and wiped the flat of the blade on her sleeve, wishing she had her whetstone. The sound of Wuranax's early arrival pulled her gaze away from Firinne.

The wyvern hovered in the air above them, holding a large parcel of what appeared to be fabric in his talons. "Found him skulking on the beach below us. Says he knows you, Seraphina?" He flew lower and dropped his bundle unceremoniously on the ground. He landed behind it and, using the claw at the joint of his wings like a hand, pulled the creature to its feet.

"Brother Reikuul?" Sera exclaimed. "What are you doing here?"

The gluxxor from Ghaia's Temple didn't answer straight away, instead brushing the dirt from off his brown robe. His cowl fell back, revealing his lizard-like face and his tongue flicked out, scenting the air. He swept his tail to the side and bowed before the gathered dragons. "It is an honour to meet you all," he intoned. "But I do not have time to properly honour you. I have come here to perform a task." He held his hand out expectantly toward Sera. "Your blade. It will need to be completely charged to do what must be done."

"Brother Reikuul... how did you know the crystals' magic needed to be replenished? I haven't used it that much since I first met you."

"Ghaia came to me on the Dreams Plain. She told me I had to help you once more."

She handed Firinne over to the gluxxor and watched as he began the process of charging the crystals. Clicking and hissing, he wove the complex pattern with his talons as Firinne hovered between them. Golden light swirled around the blade before the now-familiar flash of white imbued the runes with magic once more.

"Thank you, Brother. And... next time you're talking to her, thank Ghaia for me."

"You can thank her yourself through prayer," he gave her an accusatory glare. "The Gods have your back, Seraphina. Do not disappoint them."

Without so much as a goodbye, the gluxxor slunk into the woods, quickly disappearing into the gloom. Soon after his disappearance, the rest of the thunder returned, aside from Lylerion. As the sun was now almost at its apex, Sera announced to the gathered dragons, "It's time." Patting her sheath one last time to assure herself Firinne was still there and slipping her arms through the straps of her pack, she mentally pulled herself together. Straightening, she addressed the thunder through her mind. *This is how I'll communicate with you all if I can't speak my concerns out loud.* She took a steadying breath. *We're as ready as we'll ever be. Let's go.*

One at a time, the dragons leapt from the cliff, aside from Vera who rode with Ghalagnur. Arius knelt to make it easier for her to climb onto his back and together they dove off the edge of the cliff. Sera whooped with joy in the moment of freefall before he snapped his wings open, letting the wind catch them and carry them up and away from the ocean. They met Lylerion at the half-way point where he reported there was no sign of an ambush that he could see. Even so, when they arrived at the meeting place, they circled the clear ground, analysing the area and checking for anything Lylerion might have missed. In the past the ground had been used to grow wheat but the farmer was letting the paddock rest this season, leaving it fallow. A forest hugged the rectangular field on the southern and western sides, while an unmarked dirt road followed the other two sides. Two small crowds had gathered on the edge of the road. One was made up of humans and mythics clustered close to one another. Sera could imagine their awe and fear at seeing seven dragons flying toward them. The second group was obviously the President's guard based on their rigid formation in the shape of a diamond. Based on the colour of the uniforms, the two people in the centre were protected by both Hunters and IRC guards.

Sera cast her mind out like a net over the field and reported back, linking her mind to Arius and the other dragons. *That's Kaesus. The second person in the middle of the group is the Director of the MRO. There are a dozen guards protecting them.* She wrinkled her nose as she recognised Hunter Tyler amongst them. *The only other lifeforms I can locate are the humans and mythics that we can already see. I can't sense any underground traps or wards.*

Arius replied quickly, *There's movement further in those woods too, on the southern side. What can you make out?*

She swept her consciousness through that section of the forest. *I believe that must be the Little Birds. I recognise Urma's aura.* She gasped before gushing, *My parents are with them, as well!* The worry that had been dogging her since they'd separated eased. *They made it there safely, thank goodness.* She did a quick count. *There are about fifty auras hidden amongst the trees.* She chuckled quietly. *And there's Wren sneaking in behind them. I don't think he was supposed to be there but he's followed anyway. It wouldn't be the first time.* She released her connection to the thunder, not willing to exhaust herself too soon.

With that, Arius adjusted his trajectory and landed in the paddock, the other dragons following swiftly after.

There was a great boom when Ghalagnur landed, dust puffing up from beneath his talons. Gasps of wonder floated through the air from the gathered citizens as they gawked at them. Sera dismounted and walked to the centre of the empty field with her hands raised in a peaceful gesture. Arius followed just behind her while the other six dragons fanned out into a triangle formation with her at its head. Kaesus and the Director marched forward with their personal guard to meet her. His smug expression triggered a whirlwind of emotions as she approached her biological father. The hope and pity she'd briefly felt for him in the IRC were overtaken by rage and hatred.

Kaesus had ordered the hit on Hazel which had resulted in Idris sacrificing himself.

Kaesus had held her mother prisoner, while her loved ones believed she was dead for over twenty years.

Kaesus was responsible for the hunting and harvesting of innocent mythics since the end of the Mythic War.

*How many other families have lost loved ones because of him? How many more will if I fail today?*

# CHAPTER TWENTY-FOUR

ALL SERA WANTED WAS to unsheathe Firinne and kill Kaesus right then and there. But the earlier reasoning from her dragon family echoed in her ears, staying her hand. She channelled Talegar as she schooled her features into a poker-face, not giving Kaesus the pleasure of seeing the pain he'd caused.

Urma appeared from the tree line then, flanked by Sera's family and friends. Her heart soared at the sight of Allen, Elisabeth, Del, Hazel, Balthazar, Helena and Constantine, all walking toward the dragons. Everyone paused when an unexpected susurration reached their ears. Sera and the others shaded their eyes and looked to the heavens, the sky darkening as a massive cloud travelled at speed toward them. Sera's brows kissed. *That doesn't make any sense.*

As it grew closer, the sight of Tor, Bels, their Queen, and what looked like the entire hippogryph flock, greeted them. Before Sera had a chance to address them, the earth between the two parties shimmered and split, cracking open to reveal a tunnel. A mob of gargoyles erupted from the ground, Alistair at their head, filing out to stand in support of Sera. Out of the corner of her eye, she spotted Quill flitting surreptitiously across the field, before coming to rest in the shadow of Ghalagnur. She couldn't stop a brief smirk from crossing her lips at the President's jolt of astonishment. The opposing sides met in the centre of the paddock, the mythics taking up most of the eastern area. The security team surrounding the President shifted uneasily at the proximity of the enormous dragons.

"President Kaesus," Sera greeted him formally. "Director," she acknowledged her old boss, even though everything inside her was screaming to hurt him like he'd hurt her friend.

"Well met, Seraphina Azura," the President replied. "I am so proud of you, my daughter."

Her hackles raised at his term of endearment before confusion overtook her emotions when she processed his words. "Proud?" she asked, struck dumb by the compliment.

"You have achieved more than I could ever have imagined in such a short amount of time. It's remarkable. You're remarkable."

She bristled, angry at him for throwing her off guard with his kind words. Glancing over the group of mythics and humans who had come here for her, she searched until she found her parents. The love and pride shining from their faces brought her back to the point of the meeting. Clearing her throat, she raised her voice so it carried over the field. "We are here for two reasons. Firstly, to show the people of this great country that you have been lying to them for years about a great many things. One of your biggest secrets is the fact that dragons do still exist and you knew it. Their community has been recovering after the Mythic War in a hidden location far away from you and the Hunters. The dragons do not intend to harm humans and wish to reintegrate with our society, provided their safety is guaranteed. The other major secret you've been keeping is what really happens in the IRC. For years, you've had innocent mythics captured for false crimes and harvested for parts. You've used their bodies to perform experiments on, to find a way for humans to steal their magic."

Murmurs rippled through the gathered citizens from Mandar City at her revelation.

"I've seen this horror with my own eyes. Due to this discovery of crimes against mythics, our second reason for this meeting is to arrange for the Peace Covenant to be amended to give mythics the same rights as humans. They are sentient beings with their own culture who do not deserve the prejudice and brutality that they have been subjected to." She made sure to project her voice so that the gathered crowd could hear her demands. "I believe the first step is for you to resign and relinquish your control over the MRO and IRC. We need to set up a new government department with equal share of mythics and humans on the board to discuss how we can move forward with appropriate changes to the Covenant."

"Why should I do that?" President Kaesus said with a relaxed smile, not showing any sign of fear for the seven monstrous dragons and army of mythics in front of him.

Sera opened her mouth to respond but Sally interrupted with a lunge and a snarl. "Because I will flame you to a crisp if you don't."

Tyler and the other Hunters had their hands on their weapons in a moment, ready to shoot.

"Sally," Arius reprimanded her sharply. "We're here to foster peace, remember?"

The blue dragon backed down but kept her teeth bared.

Turning back to Kaesus after checking that Sally was keeping her fangs to herself, Sera said, "Because it's the right thing to do. Mythics have suffered under your rule since the war but not only that. Everyone who has ever spoken up for them has been silenced. We come in peace, but we will not hesitate to retaliate if you insist on pushing for war."

Kaesus held his hands up in surrender. "Calm yourselves." His tone was open and heartfelt when he spoke, but Sera didn't trust him. "There is no need for war. I'm willing to discuss your terms. To answer your accusations, I'd just like to point out that, whilst I suspected that the dragons hadn't completely died out, I had no idea there was a hidden society."

"Lies," hissed Vera, hidden behind one of Ghal's horns.

Kaesus shot a dark look toward Ghalagnur, vexed that he couldn't see the speaker. "I assumed that, so long as we kept to ourselves and didn't bother the last of the dragons, they would leave us in peace. That assumption proved true until your actions brought two dragons into the city during the Choosing Ceremony."

Sera bit her tongue, knowing he was trying to goad a rise from her, as well as turn the people of Mandar against her.

"In regards to the charge of collecting mythics for experiments, it's true."

There were cries of outrage from the spectators at his admission.

"However," he continued, his voice surging as he spoke over them, "I only did it for the good of mankind. My Alchemists have been seeking a cure for the diseases that have beset our society since the war. I'm sorry for the lawless creatures that were lost in the name of science, but I believed that helping the law-abiding citizens of Mandar took priority."

Sera crossed her arms. "So, what you're saying is, you only did what you did for the greater good?"

He studied her intently before answering with a simple, "Yes."

"That's the sign of a good politician." She gave a sardonic smile. "Always able to twist your words to cover up the most heinous of crimes. I watched you kill a hippogryph for protecting his son. I was at the trial where a shadow was falsely accused of murder. You then condemned that shadow and its child to live a life as your spy or face death. And then a harpy told me how you cut out her mate's tongue and crushed her eggs, her unborn clutch still inside. Your version of the greater good is not a 'good' that I want to be a part of."

A look of concern flickered across the President's face.

Shouts of horror met her restrained inventory of the President's many sins.

Urma added her voice to the din, shouting, "You stole my wings!"

Other voices rose in a crescendo, condemning him.

Sera spoke quietly then, and the crowd hushed to hear her words. "We can't trust you, Kaesus. And when the time comes that we can't trust our leader, it's time for a new one. You don't deserve to be in a position of power. Resign, leave this country, and we will allow you to go in peace."

More shouting met her words as the mythics who had been hurt on his orders, snarled at her offer of mercy.

Kaesus cracked his neck. "And then what?" he demanded. "Are you going to claim the position of president?"

"No," she replied curtly. "There will be others, better qualified than I, to take over the job. I wasn't made to lead a country. Only to stop the country from falling into ruin from a poisonous leader."

He glared at her, the sudden hatred in his gaze like a physical blow, forcing her to take a step back. Everything happened very quickly then. A slight movement made her eyes flick over to the Director who had remained silent and steely-faced throughout the exchange. Tyler then shifted, drawing Sera's eye, distracting her, when the Director drew his pistol from behind his back. But he was too slow to match the reflexes of a dragon. Thrusting his head forward, Arius snapped his jaws over the Director. Raising his head, he shook vigorously, essentially tearing the man's body in half. Mouth agape, Sera monitored the trajectory of the Director's body and didn't notice when the President leapt forward, grabbing and turning her in one motion to tuck her in close to his body. She bucked her hips and drove her elbow into his gut but all she got for her troubles was a grunt. His iron grip around her torso didn't yield. She was vaguely aware of the stampede of mythics toward their group but was too caught up in her own battle to see what was happening. A bright light flashed beside them and a portal opened up. Kaesus flung himself through it, taking her with him.

# CHAPTER TWENTY-FIVE

LANDING ON AN EMPTY beach, Sera tumbled free of Kaesus' hold. She jumped up and pulled Firinne from its sheath. The President was already standing and pointing a gun at her.

The harpy, Zara, closed the portal and muttered to herself, "What's one extra traveller?" Giving her wings a shrug, the harpy flashed Sera a grin, her sharp teeth making the expression far more frightening than it should be. "Oh, hey, Sera. Fabulous to see you again. I know, I know, I said I'd never come back here, but Xoran convinced me." She rolled her eyes. "I keep telling him he's far too empathetic for a harpy." She gestured toward Kaesus. "I've frozen his body from the neck down for you, so feel free to monologue if you need to get anything off your chest. He can't hurt you."

Kaesus looked between the harpy and Sera, confusion marring his features.

Zara winked at Sera before studying her clawed hands nonchalantly. "Shall you tell him, or shall I?"

Sera held Firinne threateningly, pointing the tip of the blade toward Kaesus. "Zara got her mate back when I destroyed the IRC. You killed her children. Who do you think she's going to help?"

"I own you," he snarled at the harpy.

"Not anymore, you don't," Zara replied with a snarl and leapt onto his rigid body, forcing the gun out of his hand before striking him over and over with her talons. Frozen as he was, he could do nothing to stop her attack. Blood began flowing from the wounds but as fast as the harpy made the cuts, they began healing. She paused and flicked her dark hair out of her eyes and said to Sera, "Fucking magic-stealer," she spat. "Sorry about that. I've got some pent-up rage I needed to get rid of. He's all yours."

Sera held Firinne with trembling hands, aiming the blade at his chest.

She stared down at her biological father.

She felt numb.

"Seraphina, please," he begged softly. "Don't do this."

"I have to," she whispered.

"You always have a choice."

*Was that Kaesus speaking? Or am I thinking of Allen's mantra? I mean, Dad's.*

She shook her head, desperately trying to shake away her jumbled thoughts and simply act. Kaesus was a terrible person. He'd killed so many mythics in his bid for power. He'd killed her friends. He had to die.

So, why couldn't she kill him?

"Let me help you," came another voice. The tones fluctuated between low and high and she breathed a sigh of relief as Quill appeared from behind Zara. The shadow reached out a tendril and caressed Sera's cheek. "You're not a killer, Sera. And that's okay. Will you allow me to finish the job?"

She nodded mutely, tears rolling down her cheeks as she handed over Firinne.

The shadow grasped the staghorn handle and said to Kaesus, "You arranged for my parent to be falsely accused of the murder of the human, Hector Dower. I found out the truth after Sera's escape. My parent, Inca, is dead now, because of you. I've lived my life as a slave, because of you. You have been behind the deaths of hundreds of mythics, if not more. Your daughter is the best thing you ever did in your life, and you didn't even have anything to do with her. You don't deserve the honour of life. And you certainly don't deserve the magic you stole from innocents. I can see it, you know. The magic that flows through your veins, poisoning your body. But you just keep piling more magic on top, patching up the symptoms but never fixing the source. I hope the Gods punish you for eternity. Time to die, Malcolm."

Quill plunged Firinne deep into his chest, and sickly green light poured from the wound as the magic abandoned its host. Sera closed her eyes, unable to watch the horror but she could still hear the wet gurgles of blood as her father died.

Zara beamed and pointed a clawed finger at Quill. "Now, that's how you monologue."

News travelled fast. That night, thousands more humans and mythics trekked from Mandar City to the field to meet the dragons. Zara had transported Sera and Quill back to the field and instructed Arius to burn the body of President Kaesus before disappearing into another portal. Upon her return, Sera found out that, following the death of the MRO Director and disappearance of their President, the team of Hunters and IRC guards had quickly surrendered. The Little Birds and a mythic from each species had discussed their fate and decided to offer them a fair trial at a later date. They were now confined to a makeshift prison in the forest.

Sera touched the empty sheath on her hip for the fifth time that night. She'd made the difficult decision to let Firinne burn with the President's body. The blade had served its purpose. And she couldn't help feeling she wouldn't be able to use it after it had drunk the blood of her biological father. That didn't mean it was any easier for her to say goodbye.

Arius hadn't left Sera's side since her brush with death. She knew she'd be feeling the same way in his place, so accepted his fussing graciously. Together, they wandered through the improvised festival that had sprung up. Most of the dragons had lain down to be less intimidating and spoke eloquently with their new friends. But, even stretched out on his belly, Ghalagnur was an extraordinary sight. His head alone was twice the height of the tallest human present. During the evening, two women, a gluxxor and a unicorn approached Sera to put their names forward to be part of the new department for mythic rights. Sera had no idea what she was doing but smiled and had Hazel take down their details on her PSB.

Vera flew to Sera's shoulder, interrupting her and Arius' peace. "You did good, young 'un."

"Vera doesn't give compliments easily," remarked Arius with a serious face. "Consider this a great boon, my Soulbound."

Sera studied her dragon, trying to figure out if he was teasing when Vera growled playfully. "Respect your Elders, Banished Boy. I might be small but I can still clip your wings."

Brows furrowing, Arius asked, "I thought the Elders decided to lift my banishment?"

"We did. And it is. I just like the nickname that wyvern gave you. If you're going to be smart with me, expect to get some sass back in kind."

With a chuckle, Arius bowed his head, submitting to Vera, who blew a puff of smoke at him before flying back to Ghalagnur.

Sally intruded then, with Lylerion trailing behind her. "If it's all the same to you, I will return to Sky Valley tonight. I've never been away from Corbin for this long. I miss him so much. I feel as though my heart is being torn from my chest. I will tell the Elders what happened here. I'm sure the other dragons will be curious about the humans. They're sure to return to Mandar before long." Sweeping a wing out to indicate the cream dragon behind her, she said, "Lylerion has offered to join me on my journey." She touched her snout to Sera's forehead. "Fly fierce, Seraphina. I can't wait to see you back in the valley and tell you stories of your great-grandmother. She would be so proud of you. I wish she were here to see this."

"Strike strong, Sally and Lylerion. Thank you again for your support. It means the world to me."

Lylerion bowed his head before joining Sally as they took off. A hush fell over the crowd at the splendid sight of two magnificent dragons winging their way into the night.

Sera gazed out over the celebration, the sound of laughter and chattering filling the evening once more.

*I can't believe we actually did it.*

She moved through the throng, Arius a few steps behind her, stopping to admire the various creations thrown together that afternoon. A few humans had used dye to paint a cloth with an artistic approximation of a dragon to honour their return. Sera marvelled at the simple artwork. Other than Alistair's carvings, she'd never seen anything like it since Kaesus had made sure any job in the arts had taken a backseat after the Mythic War. The string quartet from Harongar Isle that had played at the Choosing Ceremony were performing as part of the celebration. Donny, the tauron, with his cart of baked goods was giving away food to the revellers. Sera watched with a smile as her mother led Wren up to the stall and Donny gave them both a blueberry danish.

The dragons had lit small bonfires for everyone to gather around as they spoke. A news reporter was there with their camera crew spinning a positive story on the incredible development, but glossing over the fact that the President was the one who had kept the information from the citizens of Mandar. By midnight, Sera's cheeks ached from smiling and her eyelids grew heavy. Fatigue dragged at her limbs and she linked her mind to Arius. *I'm exhausted. I need to sleep. Did you want to come back to my apartment or just sleep nearby?*

*I want to stay with you. Where will you go?*

She glanced around, still not quite able to believe that they had pulled it off. She hesitated before answering. *I'm dead on my feet. If you don't mind missing out on a bed, how about you and I sleep in the forest tonight?*

*Sounds like a good plan to me,* he replied.

*I'll just say goodnight to my parents.* She smiled at the words, barely able to accept that, with the help of her friends, the Little Birds and the other mythics, they had brought around a new era of peace. She felt blessed that both her parents were alive to see it. She yawned and rubbed her eyes.

Arius nodded. *I'll give you some private time with your family. I'll be waiting for you when you're ready.* He began speaking with the green wyvern, Wuranax, as Sera walked away.

She opened her mind and winced at the onslaught of auras assaulting her senses. Singling out her mother's distinctive glow, she shut her talent down and walked towards where Elisabeth sat beside Allen on the other side of the field, speaking with Wren and Urma.

Hugging the tree line to avoid the clusters of beings around the five dragons that still remained, she found herself occasionally stumbling over tree roots. She yawned again, exhaustion pulling at her limbs. While she walked, she heard someone call her name from the shadow of the trees. She stumbled to a halt and frowned. The voice was familiar but she couldn't quite place it through her brain fog.

"Hello?" she responded. "Who's there?" She stepped away from the firelight and under the canopy of the trees. That was all it took. Her shirtfront was grabbed and she was pulled in behind a trunk, with a knife at her throat.

"Don't even think about calling for your dragon," the voice hissed. A second person in the shadows held a gun, pointing the barrel into the crowd. "Or your parents are dead." The hot breath whispering against her ear could only belong to one person. Tyler Grayson.

# CHAPTER TWENTY-SIX

EVERYTHING INSIDE SERA SCREAMED at her to break away from him. But she couldn't risk her parents' lives. Adrenaline pulsed through her veins, all vestiges of fatigue banished. The cold bite of the blade against her neck kept her from attacking the two men. *How in the name of Ghaia did he escape?*

"I wanted to have a little word with you."

"What do you want with me, Tyler?" she spat out his name, layering the word with as much venom as she could muster. "We already won." *Typical. Now, my qualms about using Firinne seem insignificant. I shouldn't have destroyed it!* Her stomach curdled at the feel of her partnered Hunter's muscular body pressed against her back.

He was shuffling awkwardly as he pushed her further into the woods. "You ruined my life," he snarled. "You know when you pulled your little stunt at the IRC? Well, I was there. I caught the edge of one of your dragon's fireballs. It's completely fucked my leg. The Alchemists are working on a remedy but it turns out, dragonfire burns aren't an easy fix. I'm a Hunter. That's who I am. But I can't hunt if I can't fucking walk. And now, you're going to pay for it."

She could feel the anger radiating through his body, making his hand tremble and nicking her skin with his knife. The trickle of blood running down her neck made her nerves scream. "How did you get out?" she asked, trying to distract him from whatever plans he had. Panic began to gnaw at her insides as they lost sight of the bonfires.

"You think you're so special," he snarled. "You're not the only one with people who care about you." He kept pushing her forward. "My parents, along with my unicorn, Madatrax, took down your guards and released us." He puffed his chest forward. "We're going to finish what the President started." Finally out of earshot of the festivities, he shoved her to the ground. She stumbled to the earth and, before she had a chance to scramble back up, Tyler's friend had her on her knees, arms secured behind her back. Kneeling in front of her, Tyler propped the tip of the blade under her chin, forcing her to look at him. "When I chose you as my Tracker, I lifted you out of mediocrity and showcased your talents to the MRO. I made you who you are. I thought we would make a great team. I thought my benevolence would make you adore me. How wrong I was." He laughed bitterly. "President Kaesus was a great leader who was fixing everything about this shitty town. He was going to employ the Hunters to rid the streets of all mythics. He might be gone, but we can still complete his mission. His only flaw was that he didn't want to hurt you. I don't have such reservations. Because you fucked it all up. Everything I've ever worked for, you've taken away. You've ruined my future, Sera. So now, I'm going to take away yours."

Tyler had made the mistake of taking her parents out of the direct line of fire. So, she had no reason not to connect with Arius' mind now, frantically screaming for aid. She sensed his terror at her cry for help. But she was too late.

In one fluid motion, Tyler pulled his knife away from her chin, raising it up above his head. Sera's eyes widened as Tyler's blade descended, as if in slow motion. She tried to throw herself backward but the second man was holding her tight. Behind Tyler's head, the silhouettes of the trees suddenly disappeared as dragons tore down the forest, seeking them. She smiled peacefully as she saw Arius' glorious scaled head appear in the distance, the moonlight painting his scales silver.

The knife hit a rib before Tyler shoved it forcefully into her chest.

*This wasn't supposed to happen,* she thought, unsure if she was still connected with Arius or simply talking to herself. She began shaking uncontrollably. Everything felt fuzzy now. A buzzing filled her ears. *Is this how I die?* She craned her neck, seeking the loving gaze of her Soulbound, but Tyler leant over her, filling her vision with his wrathful face. She didn't want her last sight of this world to be of the Hunter. She wanted her dragon.

*Arius...*

# CHAPTER TWENTY-SEVEN

## ~ARIUS~

HE SHOULD NEVER HAVE left her alone. He cursed himself, using every swear word he knew in English and Dragonish. He had been trying to give her the space she needed to reconnect with her family. He was trying to do the right thing. And look where that had gotten him. He didn't know what he'd do if he lost her. He shook his head. He couldn't afford to think like that.

*Where are you, Sera?* he blasted the thought through their tenuous connection. When he received no response, he roared his panic, startling everyone on the field. Whilst the other dragons didn't know what exactly was happening, they joined him in his destruction of the woods.

"Seraphina!" he yelled. When he still had no response, he focussed on the direction of her soul, hurriedly trampling trees as he sought her out.

*This wasn't supposed to happen.* Her voice sounded distant, as though he were hearing her underwater. *Is this how I die?* An explosion of pain whipped through the bond and he cried out.

*What's going on, Sera? What wasn't supposed to happen?* As he bounded forward, he saw the back of a man leaning over his Soulbound, pressing his blade into her chest.

*Arius...*

Time stopped making sense. He trumpeted his pain and fury into a challenge and ripped the man off of Sera, throwing him into a tree. Tyler. He should have known. Another man he didn't know was holding Sera's arms, but released her and scrambled away at the sight of the dragon. Arius threw a fireball at him, burning him alive. Arius ignored his screams and hesitated, deciding whether to scoop up Sera or murder Tyler for what he did to her.

Vera flew past his head, "I'll take care of the brüsjidt."

The tiny amphiptere flung herself at Tyler's head, and tore out his eyes. The man screamed as he tried to fight her off and she grinned wickedly, blood dripping from her maw.

As much as he'd like to watch the show, Arius turned away to ascertain the damage done to his Soulbound. "Seraphina," he spoke softly, silently begging her to open her eyes. Blood pumped from around the knife that still poked out of her body. Her chest still rose but her breathing was shallow and quick. He whimpered, raw fear overtaking every other emotion. Sensing other beings approaching him from behind, he spun around protectively, mouth open, ready to kill anything that resembled a threat. Elisabeth and Allen held up their hands in surrender. He paused his attack, reluctantly allowing them access to Sera.

Elisabeth screamed and ran to her daughter.

Allen froze for a moment, staring in horror at the sight of his little girl broken and dying on the ground. Shaking himself free of his devastation, he gave Arius a grim look. "You need to find a way to save her." Taking action, he hurried forward and took his shirt off, wrapping the fabric around the knife and applying pressure. "We need to leave the knife in for now to slow the blood loss," he instructed. "If we take it out, she'll bleed out in seconds."

Terror washed over Arius, immobilising him. He stood there helplessly, lost in the nightmare.

Aliah arrived just at that moment and cried out when she took in the scene.

Turning to his sister, Arius pleaded, "How do I save her? All this power and there's nothing I can do."

"Yes, there is! Or, at least, I think so." Flaring her wings open and closed fretfully, Aliah said, "Sally and I were discussing the prophecy. It was never written down, only spoken. What if..." she hesitated, chewing her lip, "what if 'air' is actually, 'Eyre?' Rebirth in Eyre? Maybe the prophecy knew she would die if she didn't make it to Lake Eyre in time?"

"What's the point of taking her to Lake Eyre?"

"I don't know!" she wailed. "But everything else in the prophecy has come to pass. If there's a chance..."

Arius stared at her for a long beat. "Air. Eyre. Could it be that simple?" He shook his head and gently scooped Sera's body up in his foretalons. "We don't have time to analyse it. I'm going."

Leaping into the air, he pumped his wings ferociously. Pushing his body to the limit, flying faster than he ever had before, he prayed to all Four Gods for her survival. Seraphina was his Soulbound; she couldn't die. He wouldn't let her. He poured some of his energy into their connection, praying it would be enough to keep her breathing until they reached Lake Eyre. Praying that Aliah wasn't wrong about the prophecy.

As they flew, he kept trickling his life force through their bond. His wings faltered as his energy failed from sharing his power but he pushed through, knowing he would die without her in his life. It was strange to think that a puny human he'd only known for an infinitesimal amount of time could have changed his life so completely.

It had been her destiny to change their world but who knew she would change his heart? The lake was visible now. He only had to keep her alive for a few more minutes before he would find out whether his sister's analysis of the prophecy was accurate. Fire burned in his throat but it wasn't his usual inner magic. It was the flames of despair threatening to destroy him if he lost her. At least President Kaesus couldn't do any more harm now. His only regret was that he hadn't had the chance to torture Tyler himself. Baring his teeth at the memory of the Hunter leaning over his Soulbound, he relished the thought of the pain Vera had inflicted on him. The brief distraction was welcome to keep the grief that beat on the door of his heart at bay.

Scanning the ground below him, he noted that the hippogryph nest sat empty now that the flock was in Mandar City. He swooped low in preparation to land, breathing a sigh of relief that they'd arrived at the massive lake. He landed clumsily, cradling Sera's broken body to his chest. Trying not to jostle her, he bellowed his anguish over the water, praying to the Four Gods for a sign. That was the problem with prophecies. They were never specific. What was he supposed to do now? He gently laid her unconscious body on the shore of Lake Eyre, the water lapping around her legs, while the rest of her body lay on the stones.

"Help me!" he roared desperately to the empty sky, followed by a torrent of flames.

Unexpectedly, a burst of Illundar sounded from the heavens and he threw his head up, surprised to hear the star's song at this low altitude. An unnatural mist rolled in over the lake then and a shadowy figure appeared within the fog. Arius stood over Sera protectively, still feeding her his life force. He was willing to fight whoever he had to, but knew he didn't have much energy left for battle.

"Who goes there?" he bellowed.

Lights twinkled in the mist as the creature grew closer. He squinted at the shape as they finally revealed themselves. Another dragon stood opposite him, floating just above the water. Luminescent azure feathers covered her ancient body but her wings had been cut off. She would have to be at least two-hundred-years-old but he dared not offend her by asking the question. Arius bowed low when he realised who stood before him. It was Seraphina. The Sapphire Dragon. Sera's great-grandmother.

# CHAPTER TWENTY-EIGHT

## ~ARIUS~

"PLEASE HELP HER," ARIUS croaked, legs trembling.

The old dragon offered a comforting smile. "That's what I've been waiting to do for the past seventy years."

Seraphina coiled her long body into the shallows of Lake Eyre and tenderly picked up her great-granddaughter. A tear rolled down her cheek as she took in the failing body of the young woman. "I've seen this moment play out in a vision, but it's no easier to bear now that the time has come." Her taloned hand captured the hair that had fallen over Sera's face and gently smoothed it back behind her ear. She plucked a feather from over her heart and began scribing marks on Sera's skin. As she worked, she spoke.

"When Borin and I became Soulbound, we knew neither dragon nor humankind would accept us, even with my talent to shift into human form. So, we disappeared into the mountains to be together, unencumbered by society's expectations. But Borin's partnered Hunter trailed us. My sweet Borin held me back from immediately eating Hunter Ajax when he ambushed us. Sadly, that would be the last mistake he'd make on this Earth." She loosed a heavy sigh, grief written across her face. "Borin overestimated the affection Ajax held for him. He thought their friendship would trump the Hunter's need for fame and fortune. He was wrong." A shudder rippled over her feathers. "He killed Borin, and then, before I could destroy him, stunned me with some type of electric shock. When Ajax killed my Soulbound, a piece of me died as well.

"While I lay frozen on the ground, weeping over the body of my Borin, Ajax seized the moment and sawed off my wings. He escaped, taking my wings with him, using his unicorn's magic to transport them. After the stunner wore off, I should have taken chase but I was weak from blood loss and grief. As I lay on the earth in a pool of both my Soulbound's blood and my own, I prayed to the Four Gods to end my life. Instead, they showed me the vision of this moment and one other. They showed me that, whilst in human form, Borin and I had fallen pregnant with our darling Del. She was the only reason I didn't kill myself immediately after losing my Soulbound. My heart broke that Borin would never get to meet his little girl but I vowed I would give her the best life I could. When she was born, she was a human. It grieved me greatly to know she would never feel the wind under her wings. But then, neither could I anymore. At least I had the chance to enjoy the sensation for over a century." While Seraphina continued her tale, she meticulously scratched ancient runes onto Sera's cheeks. Sera was cold to touch, her heart beating slowly and Arius fretted over the pallor of her skin. "As Del grew older I knew her best chance of living a full and happy life was to integrate into the human world. Once I found a loving family to raise my daughter in my stead, I retreated into the wild. I've been asleep for most of the past fifty years, only waking to feed, but I knew I couldn't end my life yet, for young Seraphina's sake."

Arius listened in stunned silence to the tale of self-sacrifice. He had kept trickling his energy into Sera as the old dragon worked her magic but his body couldn't give anymore without shutting down. He cut off the link and sank to his belly, beyond exhausted, and rested his head beside Sera.

Finally, Seraphina raised the quill to her own head and carved one last intricate symbol. It appeared to be a six-pointed star with two interlocking circles encompassing it and a single line running through the centre. "This will cause her pain," she warned. "But she will survive. More than that, she will thrive. She will absorb my talent. The first human to ever have two talents and be Soulbound to a dragon. Incredible." Seraphina quickly pulled the blade from Sera's chest before throwing her head back with a roar. But it wasn't the usual thunder of a dragon's call. It started out as a single, plaintive note, breaking Arius' heart. Her song soared and fragmented, mixing with the music of Illundar, creating a complex tapestry of sound. The runes on Sera's body began glowing a brilliant blue. The symbol on Seraphina's forehead mimicked it. She gave Arius a sad smile.

"Take care of my great-granddaughter."

Mystified, he watched as the great dragon shimmered before his eyes. He blinked, wondering if his vision was failing. But the Sapphire Dragon continued to fade, only the glowing symbol on her brow lingering. Her entire being turned into a blue mist and collapsed into Sera's body.

A hush fell over the lake. For the first time in Arius' life, the Illundar stopped singing.

The minuscule droplets of mist were absorbed quickly through Sera's skin, the glowing runes fading as it did.

The blood oozing from her wounds seeped back inside her body.

Colour returned to her cheeks, and she sucked in a shuddering breath.

Daring to hope for the impossible, Arius raised his head and waited anxiously for his Soulbound to open her eyes.

Then Sera's scream ripped through the night.

# CHAPTER TWENTY-NINE

*EVERYTHING BURNS. WHY IS it burning?*

Sera tore at her chest where her heart beat slowly. Too slowly. *How do I know that?*

A thousand needles raced over her body, sprouting feathers as they went. *Ghaia, please, make it stop.*

She screamed as the skin on her back ripped apart to allow the wings to burst forth. *I don't have wings.*

Clawing at her neck, she whimpered from where the flames licked her throat. *It's still burning. When will it stop?*

She curled into a ball, waiting for the end to come and weeping when everything continued to burn but she remained alive to endure it. The dawning sun's rays coloured the insides of her eyelids before the pain began to melt away. Finally, she heard it. The voice of her Soulbound, her Arius, whispering comforting words and soothing sounds in her ear as she rocked.

Raising her head, she blinked her eyes open. And flinched, cowering close to the ground in confusion. The world had changed overnight. The colours were more vibrant and everything she looked at seemed enhanced. She could hear things that were further away. Her eyes zoomed in on an eagle hunting on the other side of the lake. Not only did she hear the splash when he hit the water, but also the scrape of the fish scales against his talons.

*This shouldn't be possible.*

"Seraphina? Sera? Is it... is it you?"

"What in the Four Gods' names are you talking about, Arius?" she said with a frown. "Of course it's me." *At least my voice is still the same. At least there's one thing that hasn't changed.*

"Are you all right?" he asked hesitantly.

"My vision has gone funky and I can hear really well all of a sudden. I mean, I've always had good hearing and eyesight but this is next level. I don't mean to complain but it's freaking me out a little. Otherwise, I'm fine. Why do you ask?" Before he could answer, the memory of the night begore slammed into her. "Tyler!" she exclaimed. "He stabbed me!" Afraid of what she would see, she looked down at her chest. Sapphire-coloured feathers greeted her gaze. Completely confused, she reached up to her chest to pat them. A talon appeared in her line of sight, on the same course as her hand. Or where her hand should have been. She stared at the talon, moving each claw individually before clenching it into a fist.

"You don't know what happened after that, do you?" Arius asked gently.

She shook her head silently, a loud thudding in her ears as she tried to process the impossible.

"You were dying. Aliah and Sally figured out that when the prophecy said, 'Rebirth in air,' it actually meant Lake Eyre. So, I brought you here, praying the whole way for your survival. After we landed, your great-grandmother appeared over the lake. She performed a life-giving ritual and sacrificed her life for yours. And, it would appear, she gave you the ability to take on dragon-form."

A hundred questions flooded her mind, but the first one she asked was, "She died for me?" She dropped her head as guilt flooded her, a dark pit of despair pooling in her belly.

"Don't blame yourself. She shared her story with me and explained that the only reason she didn't kill herself after losing her Soulbound was because of her destiny. Seventy years ago, the Gods shared a vision of Seraphina saving you. She's been waiting for you all these years." He shook his head in admiration. "And just look at you." His eyes shone as they ran over her body. "You are transcendent," he whispered in hushed reverence. He extended a wing toward the lake. "Look at yourself."

Sera rose and walked toward Lake Eyre, surprised at how easily she managed on four legs. Craning her long neck over the water, she stared at her reflection incredulously. Ivory fangs peeked from between her jaws and she snapped them playfully, watching the dust motes swirl away from her abrupt action. Twisting her head to the side, she noted the tiny blue feathers flecking her snout, growing in size as they swept back along her head. Upon closer inspection with her enhanced vision, she realised that the feathers cloaking her body were many shades of blue: azure, sapphire, cerulean and a hint of cobalt beneath her wings.

*My wings!*

She flared the enormous appendages, delighting in the feeling of restrained power in them.

She turned back to Arius with a smile lighting up her face. And stopped in shock, as if seeing him for the first time. His emerald eyes captivated her completely, the tenderness in the swirling irises filling her with joy. His copper body glowed in the morning sun, with so many more tones in his scales than she'd previously realised. She could spend the rest of her life cataloguing the colours. And now she would have the opportunity to do just that.

The look of adoration on her face was mirrored on his.

They pressed their faces together, love filling their hearts while their souls soared.

"Shall we return to your family?" he murmured.

"You are my family, Arius." She winked, her unadulterated happiness making her giddy. "But, if you're referring to my parents, then yes, I'd love that. They'll be worried sick."

"They will be overjoyed that you're alive. The new look might take some getting used to, though."

Swinging her tail, she said with a laugh, "I think you might be right about that."

He cocked his head and asked, "I know this is all new for you, but did you want to try flying there?"

"Fly with you?" She met her Soulbound's gaze with a joyful smile. "Forever."

# LINKS

If you enjoyed A Dragon's Soul, please leave
a review:
altippett.com/rl/1892264

Read A. L. Tippett's best-selling series, Mother Trucking Monsters, Book One in Magic
and Motherhood:
altippett.com/rl/3566899

Claim your FREE short story when you sub-
scribe to my monthly newsletter:
altippett.com/latest-updates/subscribe/

Get to know me by visiting:
altippett.com

Or by following my socials:
facebook.com/altippettauthor
instagram.com/a_l_tippett_author
tiktok.com/@altippettbooks
bookbub.com/profile/a-l-tippett
goodreads.com/altippett

# ACKNOWLEDGEMENTS

Firstly, I want to thank you. Yes, you there, holding this book. Whether you are reading these pages on your Kindle, phone, tablet or if you've got your hands wrapped around the spine of a paperback...I want to say a heartfelt thank you for reading this story. I hope you loved reading it as much as I loved creating it.

If you enjoyed this book, please consider leaving a review. But please remember to be kind. I poured a part of my soul into these pages and, while my brain knows that it won't be everyone's cup of tea (and that's okay), my heart craves acceptance. I'm always happy for readers to reach out to me with constructive feedback; if you have any suggestions on improvements for future books please head to my website to get in touch.

Speaking of, I am so excited to share my next series, *Magic and Motherhood*, that begins with *Mother Trucking Monsters*. Make sure you check it out if you like the sound of a clumsy single mother whose life is turned upside down when a druid accidentally gives her the power to communicate with animals...and at the same time, she lands a job as an insurance assessor's assistant (say that ten times fast) but often ends up fighting magical creatures on the job! There's plenty of Australian animals, a distinct twist on cuss words, and a slow-burn romance - it's bloody **bonza**!

Now it's on to the list of thank yous...you may want to grab a drink, we're going to be here a while.

I want to sincerely thank the professionals who helped make *A Dragon's Soul* the best story that it could be.

In particular, thanks to my editor from Dana's Edits who offered wonderful insight and advice that helped take this book to the next level!

A massive thank you to my designer, MiblArt, for the stunning cover.

And a huge shoutout to Etheric Designs for the incredible chapter art!

You all rock!

Many thanks to my fabulous beta readers, Kara, Zoe, and Claire. Your feedback was so very helpful and *A Dragon's Soul* is a better story because of you.

And now, I really want to give a very special thank-you to two amazing women.

Firstly, Heather G Harris. This woman is a fantastic author and someone I've come to consider a close friend. When she's going to bed, I'm waking up, so our messages are like ships in the night. But she always makes the time to respond and offer feedback, whether that's on a cover design or a marketing plan. She's an amazing human, so make sure you check out her work.

Secondly, Andrea. My best friend since high school and now a certified superhero (A.K.A. nurse AND paramedic). I can't count how many random messages she received from me with medical questions. I probably still got some things wrong (I'm only human, after all) but it's only as good as it is because of her. Thank you, Andie!

Last, but not least:

Thank you to my parents for their unwavering support.

And, thank you to my children. It's because of you that I decided to take a chance on this writing caper.

Thank you for inspiring me to be a better person. I hope one day, when you're a bit older (and hopefully not still waking me up every night), you'll look at your Mum's achievements and be proud. I love you beyond words and beyond worlds.

Fly fierce, strike strong.

April xo

# ABOUT THE AUTHOR

I was born in the South Island of New Zealand before my family and I moved to Australia when I was two years old. We lived on a yacht for a few years and travelled along the east coast of Aussie and across the Pacific Ocean to New Caledonia. My parents schooled us via Distance Education while we sailed the seas until we bought a house on the Sunshine Coast in Queensland. I finally got to go to "real-school" and loved it – I couldn't understand why we had weekends (because, apparently, I am, and always will be, a big nerd).

Shortly before beginning high school, we moved north to a rural property near Mackay. The big draw card was that I could finally buy my own horse, a dream I'd had since I was a little girl.

Then, I started writing. I began work on my first fantasy novel when I was twelve but abandoned it after deciding that being an author wasn't a "real" job and therefore not worth pursuing. After completing my secondary schooling, my parents encouraged me to experience the real world before committing to a university degree. So, I applied to be a rider in a travelling horse show! Unfortunately, I wasn't successful so instead I did the complete opposite and got a job as an insurance broker. I worked in insurance for seven years before leaving to start a family.

I am now the mother of two wonderful children. It's tricky finding the time to write with two young kids (whilst combatting sleep deprivation!) but, thankfully, I have a Will in my life now, and he helps me find a way. I can't wait to get started on my next book and am looking forward to sharing many more stories with you!

www.ingramcontent.com/pod-product-compliance
Lightning Source LLC
Chambersburg PA
CBHW020517120726
47904CB00003B/874